# 'You are in my debt.'

'I'm sorry?'

'Yes…' Raúl's gaze encompassed her '…I'm sure you are, but not nearly as sorry as you are going to be. Because I intend to ensure that you are justly punished for what you have done.'

Nella blinked in astonishment. 'There's obviously been some mistake,' she responded.

'No mistake, Nella.'

Nella froze. He knew her name? Suddenly his threat took on a deeper significance…

**Angela Wells** was educated in an Essex convent, and later left the bustling world of media marketing and advertising to marry and start a family in a suburb of London. Writing started out as a hobby, and she uses backgrounds she knows well from her many travels, especially in the Mediterranean area. Her ambition, she says, in addition to writing many more romances, is to spend more time in Australia—especially Sydney and the islands of the Great Barrier Reef.

**Recent titles by the same author:**

DISHONOURABLE SEDUCTION

# HEARTLESS ABDUCTION

BY
ANGELA WELLS

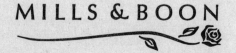

MILLS & BOON

MILLS & BOON and the Rose Device
are trademarks of the publisher.
Harlequin Mills & Boon Limited,
Eton House, 18-24 Paradise Road, Richmond, Surrey TW9 1SR

© Angela Wells 1995

ISBN 0 263 79348 6

*Set in Times Roman 10 on 12 pt.
01-9601-58602 C1*

*Made and printed in Great Britain*

# CHAPTER ONE

THE pre-dinner cocktail party was in full swing. Sipping her dry sherry, Nella smiled politely at the earnest young man who was extolling her brother's virtues to her, as if she wasn't already aware of the sterling qualities David possessed. Ten years her senior, her brother had all the right attributes required by a potential Member of Parliament, including an unblemished record in industry and a beautiful and committed wife.

Nodding her head in agreement to her companion's eulogy, Nella's mind began to wander. Uncomfortable in the undeniably chic but close-fitting dress her sister-in-law had insisted on her borrowing for the celebration of David's adoption as local Parliamentary candidate for the forthcoming by-election, she wondered how Charmian had ever managed to breathe comfortably while wearing it. She decided a little uncharitably that perhaps she hadn't, which would have accounted for her passing it over.

On the other hand, perhaps she was doing her brother's elegant wife an injustice in suspecting her of being anything less than totally generous in her intent to ensure that David wasn't disgraced by the appearance of his much younger sister wearing anything less than a designer-label frock. Besides, Charmian's upper curves weren't as voluptuous as her own, and it was possible that the older woman had found the dark turquoise moss-crêpe sheath as comfortable to wear as it was eye-catching.

5

There would be twenty guests seated in the beautiful dining-room with its long, Georgian reproduction dining-table, its gleaming surface reflecting snowy napery, crystal glasses and silver cutlery—the laying of which she had supervised earlier that day, while the florists had arranged the exquisite floral arrangements which graced the free surfaces throughout the house.

She was thrilled for David. Of course she was. It was what he wanted, and at the age of thirty-four he was young enough to make a career out of politics; provided of course, that the electorate were as impressed by his credentials as the people who had adopted him to represent them!

Again she forced her mouth into a dutiful smile as she stifled a yawn, acknowledging silently that she was as out of place in this gathering of politically activated people as snow in the desert. If she hadn't been staying temporarily at David's beautiful Devonshire house, while she was hunting around for a property of her own which she could afford to buy, she would never have been invited, she admitted wryly. With a ten-year age-gap between them, she and her brother had never been close—particularly since after their parents' divorce, shortly after her own fourth birthday, David had been sent to boarding school.

She'd offered to go out for the evening rather than cause a problem with the seating arrangements, but both he and Charmian had declared themselves horrified at the thought. More, she suspected ruefully, because her presence in their house was known locally and her absence would have reflected on their hospitality rather than because her attendance was essential to the success of the evening.

Taking a further sip of her sherry, she assumed an expression of deep interest as her companion, selected by her efficient sister-in-law as a suitable pairing for her at the dining-table, launched forth into a dissertation on the worldwide economic climate.

It wasn't that she didn't take an interest in such matters, or that Peter Fortescue was an unattractive companion. On the contrary, he was a remarkably good-looking young man, in the tradition of the well-bred English Gentleman-type, whom she suspected Charmian saw as suitable husband material for her unattached sister-in-law. It was just that Charmian's dress was too tight for her and her own high-heeled sandals were causing her feet to ache. Probably because for the past two years she'd run around in comfortable flatties while she supervised the entertainment of children on holiday at Seabeach Holiday Camp. And before that... Mentally she blocked out the past. Before that had been a stressful and painful period of her life which she preferred not to dwell on.

Also, she suspected, the air-conditioning had not been set high enough to deal with the extra heat generated by the mass of tuxedo-and cocktail-dress-clad bodies as they circulated to the accompaniment of Vivaldi and their own noisy chattering.

The sudden loud and persistent echo of the doorbell was just the excuse she needed to breathe in some fresh air. All the expected guests had arrived, so it was probably someone selling religion or house improvements. In either case she would listen politely before explaining that she was content with what she already had and dismissing the caller. In her philosophy people motivated by financial need or moral commitment should always be treated with the simple courtesy their courage and persistence deserved. She wouldn't be persuaded against her will, but neither would she slam the door in anyone's face.

Making her excuses to Peter, and indicating to one of the hired waitresses that she would deal with the caller, she made her way towards the front door. At least the interruption had given her a breathing space, both literally and metaphorically, she accorded, suppressing a smile at her own reaction as she allowed that many of her contemporaries would be enjoying this shoulder-to-shoulder contact with some of the leading citizens of the county.

Immediately she opened the door she knew her preconceived ideas had been wrong. Drastically wrong. The man whose impatient finger had stabbed continuously at the doorbell until she'd flung the door open to confront him was no salesman. Quickly her eyes absorbed his appearance. Mid-thirties, with thick dark hair tamed to a shortness which framed and enhanced a face which was undeniably and breathtakingly handsome, despite the obvious bad temper which brought dark brows furrowing over narrowed blue eyes and tightened a mouth of unremitting curves into a hard line of displeasure.

Everything about him screamed of a powerful persona. From the way he held his six-feet-plus body to the clothes which adorned it. A guest she had not been told about? Shocked into temporary silence by the apparition, she could only wait for him to open the conversation, while a quick glance from her hazel eyes assessed his clothes. A natural-colour linen jacket, impeccably tailored, covered a plain white shirt which in its turn was belted into trousers which had the colour of tree-bark and the appearance of heavy silk. The patterned tie of multi-coloured silk which blended with the ensemble and which was knotted round his strong neck found an echo in the fine, exposed line of a handkerchief in the top pocket of the jacket.

She hadn't lived the last few days with David without being able to recognise the cut of a master tailor, but on the other hand, beautiful though the clothes were, they were hardly suitable for today's celebration, which was strictly a black tie affair. Neither would the evening darkness which sculpted his firm jaw, highlighting the dimple punched out in an aggressively squared chin and emphasising the sweeping beauty of his mouth, be approved of by her brother's guests.

'So.' He broke the silence, returning her appraisal with eyes which sparkled coldly against the lightly tanned skin of his face. 'I have finally tracked you down.'

'I'm sorry?' It was as if an icy hand had been laid between her shoulderblades, only the knowledge that she was safe on her own territory keeping her standing where she was as her fingers, tightening against the door-edge, betrayed the sudden apprehension which encompassed her.

'Yes...' His gaze encompassed her, travelling from the loosely coiled pile of deep auburn hair which graced the top of her pale oval face via the tightly draped moss-crêpe of Charmian's dress to the high-heeled golden sandals which flattered her ankles to a delicate slenderness and made her slim calves flare into curves which would have delighted a sculptor. 'I'm sure you are, but not nearly as sorry as you are going to be. Because I intend to ensure that you are justly punished for what you have done to Luis.'

Nella blinked in astonishment. Obviously he was deranged. An escapee from nearby Dartmoor, perhaps? But no. Such unfortunates wouldn't have access to de-

signer clothes—unless, of course, he'd broken into a
house and helped himself...

Behind her the comforting sound of voices in conversation gave her a little courage, and some remnant
of her stern upbringing by her grandmother prevented
her from slamming the door in his face. That, and a
lingering compassion for people whose reasoning and
intellect was irreparably confused.

'There's obviously been some mistake,' she responded
with deliberate coolness. 'I've never even heard of
anyone called Lewis——'

'No mistake, Nella.' His voice was low and soft, his
tongue lingering on the double consonants, endowing
the simple contraction of her baptismal name with an
exotic flavour, deepening her first impression that despite his perfect English his mother tongue originated in
some Latin country.

She froze. He knew her name? Suddenly his threat of
vengeance on behalf of some unknown comrade took
on a deeper significance, not to be lightly dismissed.

'Ah! So now you realise I am not easily fooled.' His
startling eyes flicked contemptuously across her shocked
face. 'Petronella Esther Lambert—not a common name.
Do you deny it?'

'That it's my name? No, of course not! Why should
I wish to?'

'You really need me to tell you?' He thrust out one
hand to imprison the blade of the door, pre-empting any
desire she might have felt to slam it against him.

Nella sucked in a deep breath of air. All she had to
do was yell out for assistance. And so she would have
done if he hadn't identified her by name. Whatever his
motives, he hadn't called idly at David's door that
evening. A sixth sense warned her that it would be better

to know exactly what misapprehensions he was labouring under and attempt to persuade him of his error before she summoned help to get rid of him. The last thing David needed at such a sensitive stage of his career was a brawl on his doorstep! Despite her resolve, a shiver traversed her arms. A reaction which, she observed unhappily, didn't escape his needle-sharp perception.

'Yes, I do require an explanation,' she said firmly. 'I can assure you I've no need whatsoever to be ashamed of my name.'

'Not even the fact that you changed it? That you are no longer Petronella Esther Lambert but the Señora Luis Farrington? That you are a liar, a cheat and a thief?' The piercing stab of accusation in his voice was echoed in the clear enmity reflected in his eyes.

'What?' she gasped in shock, one hand rising automatically to her chest, as if to calm the heavy pounding of her heart. 'Is this some kind of sick joke? Who are you, anyway? Some newspaper hack trying to manufacture headlines that will embarrass my brother? Well, it won't work, because there's nothing in my background that won't stand scrutiny, and if you go around making these absurd accusations I'll sue you for slander!'

'Bravo! A splendid show of spirit!' The burning, derisive eyes slid appraisingly over her slender, defiant figure. 'When I first saw your photograph I wondered what Luis had seen in you to make him lose his head. Oh, a pretty enough face, if you like the English rose-type,' he dismissed her appearance airily. 'But my brother's taste has always veered towards the more exotic. Evidently he looked beneath the surface for once and saw the fire lurking in your spirit.' Impertinent eyes dwelt on the firm upthrust of her breasts beneath their thin crêpe covering, and every cell in her body responded to his scorn.

Slowly, he nodded his dark head. 'Yes, indeed, now I see you angry I can well appreciate the attraction. I commend his taste in flesh if not in character. But then he lacks the experience of life which would make him more discriminating in separating the gold from the dross.'

She could call for help now. Get this insulting and misinformed stranger thrown off the premises. Only that wouldn't be an easy job. He wasn't going to go quietly. Every bone of his well-balanced body was braced for conflict, every muscle tensed to fight. It was said that fear had its own scent. Well, so did anger. And the scent of this man's anger warned her against precipitate action. David had worked long and hard to be adopted by his local constituency. One breath of scandal, one adverse photograph in the paper, one hint of misbehaviour, by him or anyone in his family, could be enough to have his candidature revoked.

It was grossly unfair, but instinctively she knew that somehow she must placate this unwanted caller without involving her brother.

'Look, Mr...?' she began, forcing herself to sound composed, despite the agitation of her pulse.

'Farrington,' he supplied tightly. 'The same as my brother, naturally. Raúl Eduardo Farrington.'

Nella frowned, puzzled by the Anglican-sounding surname which followed the Latino forenames. 'Are you English?'

Bright eyes narrowed impatiently as the chiselled nostrils of his aquiline nose flared with the exhalation of a pent-up breath.

'Do not try my patience, *Señora*! You will not fool me with your childish games or persuade me that you are unaware that your husband is Venezuelan.' His contemptuous gaze condemned her utterly. 'The fact that he is a foreign national no doubt added to his other attraction—that of being in possession of a great deal of money!'

'Now, wait...' Nella interrupted impulsively. 'You can't——'

'Silence, *guapa*!' He overrode her horrified objection with the air of one who was used to commanding instant obedience. 'Neither do I doubt that your husband explained to you that our family name is of English origin because one of our ancestors was a British soldier who fought in the War of Liberation beside Bolivar, and whose name is honoured on the memorial erected in Caracas.' His light eyes, the colour of aquamarine and clear as crystal, seared across her face like lasers. 'We admire our ancestor as a brave and honest man and we bear his name with pride, but be warned, our blood also carries the pride of other races, some of which are not noted for their tolerance in the face of insult or outrage!'

'Your brother is Luis...' Mentally Nella made the spelling adjustment.

'Congratulations! You actually remember his name!' Sardonically raised eyebrows emphasised the scorn in his voice as she stayed silent, still gathering her thoughts. 'Well, I do believe we're getting somewhere at last Señora Farrington. Now, if you will stand back and allow me entrance I will tell you my plans for your future.'

'No! No—you're mistaken.' As he put the full force of his body behind his hand and pushed the door wide open, striding across the threshold, Nella fell back in dismay. 'Look—I really don't know what you're talking about,' she said quickly, the words tumbling from nervous lips as she reluctantly acknowledged that his constancy of purpose had to be rooted in some dreadful misunderstanding rather than a perverse desire to make mischief for either herself or her brother. 'Honestly, I've never met anyone called Luis, let alone married him! I've never married anyone!'

'Liar.' He spat the word at her. '*Mentirosa*! *Tramoyista!*

Horrified by the venom of the insults, Nella recoiled as his hand rose as if to strike her, feeling only marginally relieved as it stayed held at shoulder-level, palm outwards, a shocking image of threat against the beautiful cloth of his jacket.

'How dare you abuse me? Get out of this house!' Fear mingled with anger as, backing away, she found herself resting against the carved balustrade at the base of the staircase which led to the minstrel gallery. A panic-stricken glance showed her that no one was there to see her plight. Her fingers clamped against the oak support. 'If you don't leave immediately I'll call my brother and have you thrown out!'

'Why don't you do that?' he demanded with terrifying softness. For the first time since she'd set eyes on him he smiled, displaying even white teeth in a grimace which was more snarl than amusement. 'Call your brother and all his friends. Let them all learn what kind of blood runs in the Lambert veins. *Dios*!' He eyed her stormy expression with open derision. 'You are no better than a *puta*—a woman of the streets who sells her body for money. But no woman's body is worth the price you charged! Go on, *mi cuñada*, if you wish everyone to know what you have done, call for your brother! Better still, I'll save you the trouble. I'll tell him myself.'

'No, stop! Wait!'

As Raúl Farrington went to move past her Nella launched herself at him, barring his way with her body, holding out her arms to fend him off, her one thought to save David from an embarrassment which could prove disastrous.

'Ah, at last you are prepared to see discretion as the better part of valour, hmm?' Triumph etched lines of pleasure on Raúl's hard face. 'Come, we will leave immediately. The time has come to reunite you with your husband.' His hands reached out to grasp her upper arms as she heard the sound of a door opening behind her.

'Nella—what on earth is happening out here?' Charmian's light voice enquired a trifle petulantly. 'Peter said you'd gone to answer the door and disappeared. Heaven knows, we've employed enough staff for that purpose...'

Her voice trailed away as she saw the tableau before her.

'I do not deal with staff, señora.' Raúl's dark head inclined in a formed bow. 'Nella and I enjoy a personal relationship which makes that inappropriate.'

'Really?' Charmian's eyebrows winged her surprise. 'Darling, you should have let us know and we could have invited your—er—friend to join us tonight.'

'He's not my——'

Nella's protest was drowned by Raúl's deeper voice.

'On the contrary, señora. Not only would I have had to refuse such an invitation, but I regret that Nella's presence is also required urgently elsewhere.'

Charmian's beautiful face mirrored her displeasure. 'Well, honestly, Nella! You could have been more thoughtful. You know how important this evening is to David. And how am I going to explain your absence to Peter?'

'Please,' Nella appealed to her sister-in-law before her unwelcome visitor could speak, 'if I could just have a few more words in private with Mr Farrington, I'm sure I can sort something out. Ten minutes, Charmian?'

She was taking a risk, but a limited one. If she hadn't put in an appearance within the ten minutes' grace she'd requested, her sister-in-law would be certain to send someone to find her, and there was just a possibility that she might be able to use the time to convince Raúl Farrington of her total innocence.

'Very well, if you must.' Charmian nodded her elegantly coiffeured head in the direction of David's study. 'But for pity's sake, if you use the den don't touch anything. You know how fussy David is about his books, and keep it short. I expect dinner to be served in fifteen minutes!' She fixed an icy gaze on Raúl's set face before turning on her heel to rejoin her guests.

'What do you hope to do in ten minutes? Sweet-talk me? Seduce me like you did my brother?' Raúl's fingers tightened against her soft skin as he stared down into her outraged face. 'I warn you, you're wasting your time, and mine as well. Or perhaps your suggestion of discussion was just a ploy to dismiss your hostess, so that you can leave without the embarrassment of making an explanation?'

'What explanation?' Nella's frustration made her voice rise. 'Look—I've no idea what you're talking about. I'm not married to anyone—let alone your brother!'

'Then why is your name on the marriage certificate?' Triumph glowed in the summer-sky-blue of his eyes.

'There is no marriage certificate . . .' Nella's voice rose hysterically, then tailed away into silence as one strong hand released her to feel inside the light-coloured jacket and produce what was clearly a copy of precisely that.

'Did you think I was so stupid as not to bring evidence with me?' Raúl demanded scornfully. 'See, everything is here. Your so-unusual name, your address, and your father's name and profession. Rupert Sebastian— architect!' One elegant finger stabbed at the evidence. 'I think we can forgo the farce of a private discussion, don't you?'

'It's a forgery—it has to be!' Nella's hazel eyes widened in disbelief as her tormentor held the document within her range of vision but out of her grasp.

'Handed to me by the registrar himself? You'll have to do something better than that,' Raúl mocked.

The certificate certainly looked authentic. A nightmare feeling of desperation invaded Nella's heart as she sought for some entry which she could give the lie to. The place, perhaps? But no, the register office was shown as that of the large east-coast resort adjacent to Seabeach. The date, then? The first Friday in July—just three weeks ago. Dear God! Where had she been?

Desperately she cast her mind back. It had been the end of June when she'd left the camp, after having given two weeks' notice. She'd intended leaving immediately to accept David and Charmian's invitation to stay with them while she house-hunted, but there'd been a last-minute hitch with the sale of her grandmother's house, and she'd preferred to stay on in her small bed-sit in Seabeach until the cheque had come through. Grateful though she had been for the invitation, she'd had no wish to intrude into Charmian's social life for longer than was strictly necessary, or to be a burden on her relatives' hospitality at such a vital point in David's career.

With a sinking heart she realised that she'd still been in Seabeach on July the third, and that logistically she could actually have been at the register office. The resort had been crowded, and she must have seen and been seen by hundreds of people—but who could possibly vouch for her?

'The witnesses!' Grasping at straws, she stared down at two unknown names. 'I've never heard of them!'

'Of course not.' Raúl glowered at her expectantly raised face. 'What kind of fool do you take me for? Obviously with evil already planted in your heart you would have chosen two passers-by—strangers.' His tone was low now, filled with quiet satisfaction as he pocketed the document. 'Come, let's go. Your futile bleating wearies me. It's time you and Luis were reunited.'

'Wait!' Bemused by the bizarre situation in which she found herself, Nella fought desperately for a reprieve. 'There must be another way to sort out this misunderstanding and prove that someone must have been impersonating me.' As the adamantine cast of his features told her that her plea had fallen on deaf ears, she persisted spiritedly, 'Besides, you can't really believe I'd go off with a stranger?'

'Your brother-in-law,' he corrected her, undeterred by her protest. 'On the contrary, *querida*.' His sardonic tone flicked at her self-esteem with the efficacy of a ringmaster's whip. 'I believe that you will wish to avoid alienating your own brother, which would certainly be the case after I catalogue your sins before the audience of his dinner guests.' He paused meaningfully as Nella's bewildered mind struggled to make sense of her predicament. 'Because you may well be grateful for his fraternal charity after I have finished with you. However...' He regarded her pale, proud face thoughtfully. 'On one matter you are right. Despite the weaknesses of your character and the depth of your deceit you are still a woman, and physically vulnerable—circumstances which entitle you to question my credentials. Here—see for yourself.'

The quick movement of a lean hand, a flick of strong fingers and the production of a Venezuelan passport. 'Do you wish further references, *señora*?' he asked silkily. 'Would you like to speak to the Consul, or my bankers? Either would put your mind at rest about my identity.'

Nella shook her head. For what it was worth, she now believed him to be misguided rather than criminally minded, but no reference was going to make her feel any happier in his abrasive company.

'You think I am bluffing? That I won't denounce you?' If looks could kill then she would be writhing in agony at his beautifully shod feet, she thought as he lifted one darkly expressive eyebrow in open derision. 'Don't make the mistake of underestimating me, *guapa*. If you force me to, I shall tell your brother and his important colleagues everything. How, after seducing Luis into making you his wife, you persuaded him into opening a joint bank account with the money entrusted to him for business, and at the first opportunity withdrew the lot and disappeared. Your shame will be his shame.' He paused briefly, then added softly, 'And his shame will destroy him.'

'Some woman did that to your brother?' Nella's thoughts fragmented as she tried to juggle what she had heard into some kind of logic. So that was what Raúl had meant earlier when he'd referred to her as a liar, a cheat and a thief! Staring into his uncompromising face, she felt her heart flip. There was no way she could allow him to make such accusations against her in public. Not when David's future public career was at stake.

'Some woman called Petronella Esther Lambert,' he agreed tautly. 'And now you are aware that I know the full extent of your deception, you may make your excuses to your hostess and we shall leave. Your place is at your husband's side.'

It was at that moment that a streak of daylight dawned on Nella's confused mind, to be followed by a great wave of relief which spread through her veins with welcome alacrity. Dear heavens! How stupid she was being. All through this ridiculous argument she'd been aware of an incongruity, a niggling thought at the back of her mind. Now she knew what it was. All she had to do was confront Luis Farrington face-to-face. Whatever the final explanation turned out to be, he at least would know she wasn't the woman he had married!

'Where is Luis?' she asked boldly, adding anxiously as another thought assailed her, 'You're surely not intending to take me back to Venezuela?'

'Not yet.' There was pain in the blue eyes and another emotion she couldn't register. 'It seems your husband was so distraught when he returned to London and found both his apartment and his bank account empty that he set out to find the woman who had robbed him of his purse and his pride. Unfortunately he was so distraught by your perfidy that he didn't concentrate as much as he should have done on his driving.'

Oh, dear God! Nella stared back into Raúl's rigidly controlled features, her imagination making her fear the worst. Whatever his misconceptions about her, she couldn't prevent a surge of pity for his barely concealed pain.

'You mean, he's...?' Her voice died away as she found herself unable to utter the final word.

'Dead?' Raúl had no compunction in filling the silence. 'No, unfortunately for you, Nella, you are not a rich widow. Luis is in hospital in Exeter. Perhaps it will give you some satisfaction to know that he's been calling out your name—whether to condemn or forgive you is anybody's guess.'

'How can you be so callous?' White-face, she allowed her gaze to dwell on his granite countenance. 'Have you no affection for your own brother?'

'More, it appears from your reticence in accompanying me, than you have for yours,' he riposted swiftly. 'Come, make your farewells to your family or take the consequences. I grow tired of waiting.'

What options did she have? Quite apart from concern for David's future, she was experiencing an angry curiosity to discover who had had the temerity and opportunity to steal her identity and abuse it in such an appalling way, and the first step to collecting clues would be to talk to Luis Farrington.

Her mind made up, Nella nodded her head briskly. 'Very well,' she said coolly. 'Since you give me no other option I'll allow you to take me to Luis's bedside.' Turning on her heel, she walked swiftly from the room, aware that Raúl was only a couple of paces behind her as she made her way to the reception room to apologise for her forthcoming unavoidable absence from the celebrations.

A small smile curled the corners of her full mouth. Nothing, she thought gleefully, was going to give her greater pleasure than seeing Raúl Farrington's face when he was forced to admit that she had been more sinned against than sinning. Clearly he wasn't a man who was used to grovelling. Before she was finished with him, she'd make sure he ate humble pie—and in great quantity.

# CHAPTER TWO

HE WAS driving a Jaguar. A mean, lean beast of a car the colour of the deep sea on a stormy day, with a capacity for speed far greater than the legal limit. Nella sat silently beside Raúl, her jaw clenched firmly, her eyes fastened on the road ahead as the needle on the speedometer rose.

Irritated at first, when Nella had started to make her excuses, Charmian's attitude had changed instantly when Nella had told her she'd been summoned to the bedside of a friend injured in a motorway smash, insisting that she didn't hurry back from the visit and, if she preferred, that she stay in a hotel near the hospital.

David, too, had been sympathetic, urging her to telephone him when she'd seen her friend if she needed any help—financial or otherwise. It was lucky, she opined, that both her brother and his wife had been too occupied with the party to enquire too deeply into the circumstances. But she'd made sure they knew both Raúl Farrington's name and the registration number of the Jaguar.

Her taciturn companion had made no attempt to stop her providing such information. In fact he'd gone out of his way to provide further proof of his credentials, even suggesting that David made a note of his passport number and London address and telephone number as a sensible precaution.

Nella sighed. She didn't doubt her abductor was genuine; he was a predator caught in the same incredible

22

trap as herself, oblivious to everything but his own desire
for revenge, but genuine nevertheless.

She shifted in her seat, staring out of the window as
the sun sank lower in the July sky. The heat of the early
evening was giving way to the balmy warmth of a summer
night, and she certainly felt a lot more comfortable now,
dressed in pale cream trousers topped by a sleeveless
cream satin V-necked blouse covered with a loose edge-
to-edge jacket in cinnamon-coloured silk. She'd bought
the blouse and trousers in a high street store, and had
been pleased enough with them, but the jacket had been
a real find. She hadn't really believed that designer
jackets sometimes turned up in charity shops for a few
pounds, but then she supposed it depended where one
lived—and David lived in a very up-market area.

Her thoughts turned to the stranger she was about to
visit. How badly hurt was Luis? she wondered. Her brow
creased into a frown. Should she ask the man sitting
beside her or would that prompt more abuse from him?

'Regretting you missed the party?' He was concen-
trating on the road, tossing the question at her without
a glance in her direction. Perhaps he'd caught a glimpse
of her worried face in the mirror, she surmised. 'Hoping
to find some other rich *idiota* there to augment your
bank balance, hmm?' He didn't wait for a denial. 'Only
Luis isn't a rich man. What you helped yourself to was
company money, which he has no means to replace, but
I suppose it didn't matter to you that he might face imprisonment for embezzlement on his return to Caracas?'

'No, it didn't,' Nella agreed calmly. How could it have,
when she'd never even met the wretched Luis? But it was
pointless to keep repeating that fact. A perverse sense
of mischief born of frustration tempted her to refrain
from further protestations. After all, it couldn't be much

longer before the face-to-face meeting with Luis cleared her entirely of all implication in the disaster which had befallen him.

She forced herself to relax in the comfortable seat. At the speed they were travelling it wouldn't be too long before they made Exeter, then all her problems would be resolved. No, that wasn't quite accurate. She frowned. It would be a simple matter, given Luis Farrington's endorsement, to establish that she had never set eyes on him before, let alone gone through a marriage ceremony with him, but it might be more difficult to discover who had got hold of her name and particulars—and used them illegally in such an embarrassing way. Obviously it was a matter which would have to be dealt with with the utmost speed, so the records would be put straight. Discreetly, too, if David wasn't to receive unwelcome attention from the Press.

'You thought I would bail him out, I suppose?' The harshly voiced question drew her attention back to the man beside her. His firm profile with its strong nose promised her no mercy; only the soft cleft in the granite chin appeared to humanise him. 'Well, so I have. Every pound has been repaid into the bank, so you are no longer in his debt. The alternative for you is perhaps more alarming—because you are now in mine.'

'If you say so.' Nella shrugged her shoulders, determined not to enter a futile argument. Over the past two years it had become second nature for her to accept a regular mantle of guilt, if not gladly at least with resignation!

'Oh, I do say so.' The odd gentleness of his voice was more disturbing than if he'd raised it. 'I only hope, for your sake, that you still have most of your plunder intact.'

'Most being what?' she asked resignedly. It was one way of passing the time and it was beginning to amuse her, in a warped kind of way, to draw him on towards his own destruction. Dear heavens, how was she going to enjoy seeing Luis Farrington's blank stare when she walked into the ward.

'Trying to fool me, Nella? It won't work, *querida*. You may have been able to deceive and seduce my brother with your pale skin and innocent eyes but, believe me, you've met your match in me. I have already made my enquiries at the London branch of my brother's bank and confirmed the details I was able to piece together from the evidence left in his apartment. Twenty thousand pounds you stole from him, and you're going to repay each one with interest.'

'Twenty thousand!' She was too shocked to conceal her surprise. No wonder he'd acted so arbitrarily and with such resolve. Perhaps if someone had stolen that amount of money from someone she cared for she would have played judge and jury too. Only *she* would have made sure she identified the real culprit first.

'Don't even try to deny it,' Raúl retorted flatly. 'I have all the proof I need. Luis phoned me in Caracas a week after he'd married you, to inform me of what he had done and to ask me to break the news gently to our mother.' He shot her a sideways look loaded with venom. 'Such a glowing description of the "English beauty whom you will love as dearly as I do when you meet her". I expect you knew all about that—perhaps even stood beside him while he sang your praises?'

Nella sighed. 'No, I——'

He broke into her weary denial, his voice harsh with a simmering anger. 'Ah, but it didn't take long before he discovered the truth, did it? And then, as usual, his first thought was to enlist my help to get him out of trouble.

'When he returned to London after his business calls in the north and discovered your treachery he started to write a letter to me, to put his agony into words. But he abandoned it in crumpled sheets of paper as his emotions overran his skill of explanation, and he decided instead of enlisting my help to set out on your trail by himself—determined to find and confront you with the crimes you'd committed against him.' His jawline clenched as his voice grew harsher. 'When I received news of his accident I left Caracas to be at his bedside, but first I went to his apartment in London with the intention of consoling and helping his wife of a few days— even though I disapproved of the liaison.' He cast her a withering glance. 'That was where I found the crumpled pages of the letter detailing your treachery.'

His strong, beautifully shaped hands tightened on the wheel as Nella drew in a sharp breath, nervously aware of the latent power they commanded. How glad she would be when they reached Exeter and her innocence was proved. She'd no wish to be this man's sworn enemy for a moment longer than necessary.

As if sensing her sudden fear, he flung her a scathing glance, stripping his eyes down her face as if he were peeling paint from a wall.

'Oh, you may well have qualms now, *querida* ...' The endearment, like those which had preceded it, was spoken with a scalding scorn. 'Because, disjointed and incoherent as the letter was, I managed to piece the whole sad story together. The deliriously happy three-day honeymoon the two of you enjoyed before Luis had to get on with the job he was being paid to do. Your decision not to go up north with him but to stay in London

to get your passport renewed and to buy a trousseau for
your new life in Caracas.' He paused and Nella's nerves
tightened a notch.

When he resumed, his voice was quiet, almost soft,
but each syllable was enunciated clearly, as if he were
punching it like a nail in a coffin—her coffin.

'Money. You needed money, you told him, to enable
you to dress as befitted the wife of an executive of his
stature. Hah!' His bark of harsh laughter echoed round
the car. 'A marketing executive, and you treated him as
if he owned the company. No wonder he was flattered!'
He slanted her a narrowed stare from ice-blue eyes. '*Did*
you think he owned the company?' His mouth curled
derisively, anticipating her disillusionment. 'Poor, deceived Nella—if I had a heart it would bleed for you,
as Luis's did. He was besotted by you, bewitched by
your pale skin and your lush red mouth, the copper brilliance of your hair as startlingly beautiful as the waters
of Lago de Maracaibo at dusk...'

Nella sucked in her breath as the evocative words
spilled over her like hot sauce over ice-cream, meltingly
sweet but dangerous, damaging—and surely unmerited.

'Luis's words—not mine.' As if she'd ever doubted it,
despite the intensity with which he'd spoken them. 'He
was mesmerised, hypnotised, and he lost his head. He
gave you access to everything he had, by the simple
means of transferring the company's money, with which
he'd been entrusted, into a joint account. A week later
you gave notice to the bank that you wished to withdraw
the lot in cash, and the following day they opened especially for you at eight in the morning and handed it
over to you in the manager's office. This I have already
confirmed, before setting out on my own mission to
find you.'

Defiantly Nella stared at him, aghast at what she'd heard, but totally unable even to begin to deny her own implication in what had happened. Where to start? Whom did she know who could and would abuse her name in such a way? No one. She knew no one who was as mercenary and evil as the woman who had stolen her persona, and the realisation terrified her.

'Which,' he was continuing, with a menacing softness which chilled her blood, 'makes you the most expensive whore it's ever been my displeasure to meet.'

Nella flinched from the undeserved insult, her mind drowning in a flood of incoherent thought. For the second time in her life she'd been plunged into playing a part in a fantasy which was none of her choosing. Forced to accept a role where logic and common sense no longer existed, where day was night and night day; where time was a continuum of unrelated events which offended logic and challenged sanity. She'd really believed that the healing peace of Seabeach and the uncomplicated affection of the children she'd tended had been the anodyne she'd needed after the trauma of caring for her grandmother during two years of increasing dementia.

The sensation of being flung headlong into a nightmare scenario was suddenly too much for her. Uttering a sharp cry of protest, she lifted her long, slender fingers to her head, lacing them into her wealth of red-gold hair as if she could protect her brain from Raúl's bitter accusation.

'You may well cringe.' His deep voice berated her relentlessly. 'What have you done with your wedding-ring? Sold it?' He didn't wait for an answer but continued brutally. 'What were your plans, I wonder? Did you intend to wait until Luis returned to Venezuela, then set about trapping some other poor, besotted fool?' He was staring ahead, his eyes narrowed, his jaw tense. '*Dios*! But you'll rue the day you tangled with my family!'

'I already do!' The words tumbled from Nella's lips, bravado coming to her rescue, helping her conceal the surge of fear his words had engendered, realising too late that her exclamation could be translated as an admission of guilt. When Raúl's head turned briefly to observe her she had to make a determined effort not to cower away from him.

Attack was the best method of defence! Somewhere she'd read that, and heaven knew she needed to erect some barriers against the barbed accusations of her companion. She certainly held no brief for the woman who must have impersonated her, but neither was she going to allow the brute beside her to flay her alive. The prospect of having him kneel at her feet begging forgiveness in the near future was a heady stimulus. In the meantime, it might not hurt to needle him a little. She felt sorry for Luis. He had been abnormally stupid, but then it couldn't be easy having a brother like Raúl laying down the law at every turn.

She made a concerted effort to compose herself before easing her body so that she could stare at the formidable profile presented to her. Raúl Farrington was astonishingly beautiful, she decided in a detached kind of way, but it was a predatory beauty, like that belonging to an eagle or a carnivorous animal: all bone and muscle and tight skin, a physique honed to perfection, because in the jungle only the fittest survived. And instinct told her that he was a denizen of the jungle—metaphorically if not literally. Perhaps literally as well. She knew nothing about Venezuela except—her brow wrinkled in thought—didn't jaguars roam in the jungles there? Not the me-

tallic, alloy-wheeled kind in which she was now seated,
but the lean, hungry cats which prowled the undergrowth and killed at will?

'You called me a thief.' She broke the silence
conversationally. 'But a joint holder of a bank account
has every right to make withdrawals from it. There's
nothing illegal about that.'

'You abused my brother's generosity. His criminal
generosity.'

'If that were the case, then it's between Luis and
myself,' Nella suggested, greatly daring as she sensed his
reluctant acceptance of the point she'd made.

'It wasn't his money to give, which makes you an accessory to theft.'

'But you've restored the money to his account,' she
countered sweetly. 'So, even if I was an accessory at the
beginning, by replacing the amount withdrawn you've
wiped the slate clean.'

'On the contrary, *querida*, you are both in my debt.
And believe me, I intend to extort a far sterner penalty
than any court of law.'

'Whatever you say.' Nella turned her gaze to the side
window. In all fairness, although his attitude infuriated
her, she could understand how he felt. She froze, an odd
feeling assailing her, as her breath caught in her throat.

The car was no longer on a main road, but cruising
down a country lane beneath a canopy of English oaks
and sycamores. A quick glance at the set profile beside
her told Nella nothing. Even if Raúl Farrington was a
stranger to the country he was obviously an experienced
and competent motorist. He could hardly have strayed
off the main Exeter road unknowingly, neither did he
have the temperament, she suspected, to take the
'prettier' alternative route.

Apprehension tightened the muscles in her throat as she forced herself to swallow. Despite her resolve, it was all she could do to keep her voice steady.

'Where are we going?' she asked, the hammering of her heart making her feel faint. 'I thought you said Luis was in hospital in Exeter.'

'So he is.' Raúl spun the steering-wheel, turning the Jaguar into a left-hand turn down a twisting, unmade road. 'Relax, *querida*. Your reunion with your husband has merely been delayed, not cancelled. Visiting hours are over for today.' They were travelling more slowly now as the narrow lane wound in tortuous bends between high hedgerows. 'Ah! Here we are!'

They'd turned onto a narrow track and through what appeared at first sight to be a gap in a hedge, to halt on a pebbled forecourt in front of a detached, two-storeyed cottage. He applied the handbrake and turned off the ignition, before unfastening his seat-belt and turning in the driver's seat to blast her with an ice-cold stare from his startlingly pale eyes.

'We've got a lot to talk about, you and I, *mi cuñada*,' he told her softly. 'It took me several hours to locate exactly the right kind of property I needed, but God was good to me. Miles from civilisation, no telephone and no intrusive neighbours, but an excellent security system. Deadlocks on all doors and windows. A veritable prison, *querida*. A taste of what might be in store for you if you don't co-operate. Shall we go in?'

If she didn't wish to spend the night in the car it seemed she had little alternative, but her limbs seemed to have turned to aspic and her fingers to have lost all power as she remained where she was, trying to bring the rapid beating of her heart under control by sheer willpower.

'Out!' A narrow smile did nothing to soften the stern bones of Raúl's face as, having walked round to her side of the car and opened the passenger door, he reached inside, stretching across her to release the catch of her belt before taking a firm grasp on her arm and hauling her from its comfortable confines.

'I can't spend the night here!' Shock and despair had held her silent until then, but as Raúl thumbed the car alarm system, to be rewarded by a flash of lights and a soft bleep, Nella sprang to her own defence.

'Why?' He was towering over her, every primed muscle a threat to her safety. 'You think it too primitive for your taste, hmm? But appearances can be deceptive, can they not, *mi puta bella*? You may take my word for it that I have seen and approved the interior. It is entirely suitable for my brother's wife.'

His answer hung on the still air, intimidating in its directness, yet hiding within it the excuse she could use.

'That's just it,' she blurted out through stiff lips. 'What will Luis say when he finds out that we've spent the night here together?'

'What should he say?' His glance was rapier-sharp, impaling her like a skewer thrust through a lamb kebab. Even so, she was unprepared for his next move. Too late she tried to evade him as his arm shot out towards her to curl round her body beneath her armpits, dragging her unwilling body hard up against his own. 'What should he say, Nella?' he repeated, his breath rasping, his lips parted in a snarl to reveal perfect white teeth gritted together.

Somewhere a blackbird sang, a last paean of joy before dusk—or was it a cry of warning? With Raúl's fingers imprinting their warmth against her ribs, the subtle, spicy scent of his body invading her air-space, his dangerously beautiful eyes searing into her own, as if to pierce her mind and extort its secrets, Nella moaned a protest.

Two years of nursing, humouring and weeping in secret for her dearly loved grandmother in the final throes of Alzheimer's disease, followed by a similar period playing with the children of Seabeach or isolated in a lonely bed-sit as she translated the outpourings of a handful of top-class European writers into English for an up-market London publisher, had hardly prepared her to deal with a man of Raúl Farrington's powerful personality. Not only personality, she realised faintly, struggling futilely in arms which held her like iron bands containing a barrel—confining, bruising, merciless—but sexuality.

Confined by a fate which had seen her parents divorce when she was four years old, her father disappear from her life altogether, her mother emigrate to and later marry in Australia and her brother sent to boarding-school while her mother's widowed mother accepted charge of the bewildered toddler which had been herself, somehow she'd missed out on meeting presentable young men. Not that Raúl Farrington was presentable—far from it! Dangerous, cruel, vindictive... Those were the adjectives which sprang more readily to mind...

Gathering the last shreds of her strength, Nella raised her hands, pushing as hard as she could, her palms against shoulders which tensed to oppose her with an adamantine hardness.

When his head swooped forward the pressure against her wrists became unbearable, so that she dropped her hands with a small cry of pain as her tear-filled eyes rose to challenge him in angry outrage.

It was a bad mistake. Somehow he managed to transfer his grasp so that his hands pinioned her sore wrists behind her back as his mouth covered her own in a rapacious act of possession, muffling her protests, stilling her tongue, punishing her with an absolute power which left her shaking and speechless.

As he released her arms Nella stumbled backwards, her progress halted by the Jaguar. Automatically her hands rose to support herself, her fingers leaving their prints on its shiny surface, as she fought to regain her breath.

He was standing there watching her through narrowed eyes, his expression unreadable, the strong curves of his mouth damp and warmed by contact with her own. '*Ramera*!' he breathed insultingly. 'You think my brother will suspect I've sampled the trash he paid a fortune for if I keep you here with me? You think Luis knows so little about me that he will believe for one moment that I could be seduced by the face of an angel plastered on the body of a harlot? How little you know about my family!'

'I know more than you think!' Driven to extremes by his continuous barrage of contempt, Nella experienced an untypical urge to enter combat as her stormy eyes accosted his, resentment flaring. 'For instance, I know that you and Luis are not as close as you would like to believe, or he would have told you of his plans *before* he got married—even invited you to attend the ceremony—rather than wait until afterwards, when it was a *fait accompli*.'

'He knew I'd have stopped at nothing to prevent it!' Raúl snapped. 'Even if it had meant flying immediately to England or arranging for his immediate recall to Caracas.'

'You consider yourself your brother's keeper, then?'
A glimmer of cynicism deepened the honey lustre of
Nella's eyes.

'Since our father died I have assumed that role, yes.'
He regarded her with merciless eyes, apparently unaware of her sarcasm. 'Luis has many excellent qualities, but discernment where women are concerned and
a sense of responsibility are not among them.'

'Perhaps if you'd trusted him more and disciplined
him less he might have acquired them by now?' she suggested caustically.

'You dare to blame me because Luis was ingenuous
enough to play the part of Don José to your Carmen?'
Raúl regarded her, incredulity in every line of his face,
as he added grimly, 'My only fault was in not preventing
his departure from Venezuela in the first place. He was
too immature for such an appointment. Unfortunately,
I hoped it would make him grow up a little.'

'In the circumstances, one might say it did,' Nella
suggested equably, and immediately regretted her levity
as one long stride brought him before her. With a
strangely gentle gesture he lifted one hand to run his
fingers through her tumbled hair, before closing his fist
in it. 'And if you are thinking of trying to entrap *me* in
the same way, in an attempt to escape the retribution
you deserve—forget it! I'm made of sterner stuff.' The
gentle pressure against her head warned her not to dispute
his claim. Not that she had any intention of so doing.
If she'd wanted to place him in the cast of *Carmen*, it
would have been as Escamillo, the strutting, vainglo-
rious, womanising bullfighter, she thought bleakly, not
the gentler, love-smitten soldier to whom he'd likened
his brother.

'Are you listening, Nella?' His perceptive gaze swept across her mutinous face. 'Women like you are two a *bess* in the backstreets of Caracas. Even if you weren't my *cuñada*, and therefore barred to me, I wouldn't soil my body by possessing you!'

His voice said one thing but his eyes said something entirely different! Nella squirmed as he brought his face closer to her. Turning her head, she fought to evade his predatory mouth as it sought her own, gasping in shock as he slammed his body against hers and she was pinned by the vigour of his hard thighs against the polished bodywork behind her.

'*Cerdo!*' she yelped, resorting to his own tongue to return the insults he'd heaped on her own head, regretting that her vocabulary of abuse was so limited and wishing disloyally that the writers she translated were less literary and more vernacular in their output. '*Imbécil!*'

She relished the quick blink of his eyelids which registered his surprise at her lapse into his language, and was on the point of attempting to kick him on the shins when the silence was shattered by the car alarm responding to the pressure of their bodies.

To be deafened momentarily was a small price to pay for being given the means to escape! As Raúl shot away from her, fumbling for the siren control on his keyring, his mouth forming words which thankfully she was unable to lip-read, Nella dived towards the cottage, her hands clasped over her ears to protect them from the raucous decibels.

It was over in seconds—the silence almost as shocking as the original noise. For several moments she wondered if it had left her deafened, then decided that more probably it had simply frightened away every other living creature in the vicinity.

The sound of Raúl's feet crunching on the gravel confirmed her assessment as he came towards her. She regarded him warily, thankful to see that whatever emotion had been driving him appeared to have subsided and he'd become once more the stern, cold man who had disrupted David and Charmian's celebration party. She glanced down at her feet, neatly shod in flat-heeled shoes which matched her trousers, to hide the whimsical smile which she felt playing about her mouth.

At least she'd found out one thing. If Raúl Farrington's undertaking not to violate her body seemed to be under pressure, his ardour could be dampened by noise as effectively as by a cold shower! It wasn't a discovery she intended to share with him.

Opening the front door, he stood back politely, bidding her enter. She obeyed, stepping across the threshold into a pleasantly light and airy hallway. It wasn't a situation she relished but it seemed she had no alternative. No change of clothes, no toiletries ... and sharing a house in the middle of nowhere with a man who believed she'd been spawned in hell. But only for one night, she consoled herself. Tomorrow she'd meet this Luis face-to-face, and then who would be on his knees begging forgiveness?

# CHAPTER THREE

'STEAK, eggs, bread, butter, milk...' Raúl had preceded her to a small but adequately furnished kitchen, and was pointing out the main contents of the fridge. 'The freezer should be well stocked also...' Stooping slightly, he jerked the lower door of the fridge-freezer open, nodding his approval as he eyed the contents. 'Yes, everything seems in order. Also you'll find the cupboards should be stocked with other basics, like coffee and sugar. The agent appears to have followed my instructions most efficiently.'

'My, you have been busy.' Nella regarded him sourly as he inspected the wall cupboards, presumably finding everything to his taste.

'Very,' he accorded drily. 'Since receiving the news of Luis's accident, I've had to rearrange my business plans, spend eight hours in a plane, and drive God knows how many miles backwards and forwards across the southernmost part of your country, from Seabeach in the east to Exeter in the west, in my successful search for his reluctant and dishonest wife. All that with very little chance to catch up on my sleep and sustained only by the peasant food served in your motorway service stations.'

'My heart bleeds for you,' Nella murmured. 'I should have thought you would have stayed at a good hotel in Exeter rather than go in for self-catering in the countryside.'

'And allow my slippery little sister-in-law to slide through my fingers?' Contempt chilled his tone as he turned away from the cupboard to scan her questioning face. 'Besides, it was never part of my plan to support you in luxury while your husband recovered. Neither did I intend to give you the opportunity for flight. This may be a comparatively comfortable prison, but one from which you will not easily escape, I think, little bird,' he advised her grimly. 'Besides, who said anything about self-catering? The natural order of life is that the man provides and the woman prepares and serves. As you see, I've provided amply for dinner tonight for both of us. It shouldn't take you too long to grill a fillet steak. You'll find me in the main living-room when the meal is cooked.'

'And suppose I tell you I can't cook?' Defiantly Nella stared back into his presumptuous face, disliking him intensely. He was arrogant, prejudiced and totally without compassion. Stilling the small voice within her that suggested that in view of the bizarre circumstances concerning the misuse of her identity his reasons for doubting her were logical, she forced herself to meet his cold regard without flinching.

'Then I should say this is a good time to learn, *querida*. There are other ways to reach a man's heart, but since, in view of our close relationship, those are denied you as far as mine is concerned, you can make your life a great deal more comfortable by choosing the culinary way.' He stood there, running the palm of his hand across his incipient beard, the expression of cold distrust in his glacial eyes distinctly unfriendly.

'Feed the brute, hmm?' Nella forced herself to laugh. Why waste her breath in trying to persuade him that she wasn't his brother's defecting wife, when all would be made clear the next day? Let him be the architect of his own misfortune! She would have the last laugh—and the longest. The thought brought genuine amusement to shine through the clear hazel of her eyes. Time enough to sort out who had impersonated her when the first hurdles of misidentification had been cleared.

Something vibrant and dangerous sparked in the discerning gaze which had never left her face. 'A brute, eh? How perceptive of you, Nella.' Raúl accepted her intended insult as if it had been intended to flatter, the deep timbre of his voice edged with cream. 'Let's hope you never forget that fact. Because unlike my brother, who is a charming and domesticated animal, my instincts are those of the *llanos*. Kill or be killed. And I find life too sweet to wish to embrace death too soon.'

'Then I suggest you control your killer instinct,' Nella advised his retreating back, 'because in a civilised society the law avenges itself on those who abuse it!'

'My point exactly!' Turning on the threshold, he bathed her in an insincere smile which showed to advantage the peerless perfection of his teeth but did nothing to soften the adamantine hardness reflected in his gaze.

Damn the man! Nella thrust her fingers through her hair. Already coming adrift from its loosely pinned mooring on the top of her head after the journey, now the ends bounced away from her crown to fall in a mid-shoulder-length tumble down her back. She'd walked into that one, she accorded ruefully. That was what came of being innocent. Tomorrow couldn't come too soon. For a few seconds she stood still, relishing the promise of revenge. Renewed images of a penitent Raúl begging forgiveness for maligning her sent shivers of joyful anticipation through her nervous system.

Oddly, for all the ordeal to which she was being subjected, she felt more vibrantly alive than she had for the past four years. True, she'd lost the verbal battle she'd waged with the aggressive Venezuelan impatiently waiting to be fed in the next room, but at least she'd used a small amount of verbal dexterity in argument.

Not since she'd had left university to care for her grandmother—poor, darling Rosie—had she indulged in such a stimulating conversation. She'd delighted in the children at Seabeach, and she certainly hadn't spoken down to them, but the level of conversation had been far beneath that of the university debating society. Not that her altercation with Raúl Farrington would have made headlines! But it had done something to rouse her from the mental lethargy which had been affecting her for so long.

A slight smile curving her full lips, she slid her arms out of her jacket, hanging it carefully over the back of a chair as she took stock of the kitchen. At least he hadn't condemned her to some kind of hovel and set her the task of putting it to rights. The place was spotless. Brute he might be, but Raúl Farrington would always put his own creature comforts first.

She eyed the two pieces of fillet steak, impressed by their thickness. Easy enough to grill under the electric grill of the neat oven provided, she supposed, although it wasn't a cut she was used to cooking. The level of their 'doneness' was going to be largely a matter of luck, she decided, so there was little point in asking him for his preference.

The freezer revealed oven chips and a packet of frozen mixed vegetables. All in all, a quick and easy meal. Better with a sauce *au poivre*, but the store cupboard was lacking the ingredients; besides, she'd neither the time nor inclination to demonstrate her accomplishments as a cook.

Back home in David's beautiful detached house the dinner party would be in full swing. Waiting for the grill to heat, Nella basted the steaks with a light coating of oil as mentally she went through the menu Charmian had selected: mushrooms *à la* Grecque, followed by duckling with pineapple, served with mangetout and Parisienne potatoes, washed down by an excellent claret and finished off with a dessert of iced zabaione. Prepared, cooked and served by caterers, of course. Compared to that, fillet steak was rather basic!

Half an hour later, as she carried the loaded tray into the living-room, Nella decided that one of the penalties she might extort from her deluded kidnapper, when she'd been exonerated from all suspicion of having duped his brother, would be that he bought her an excellent and extremely expensive dinner at a top-class restaurant.

As Raúl rose to greet her and take the tray from her, the first thing she noticed was that he'd shaved. The second that he'd laid a small oval table by the window with place-mats, cutlery and two wine-glasses. Placing the plates on the table, he nodded to her to take her seat as he propped the empty tray against the wall and produced a bottle of Cabernet Sauvignon from the sideboard which stretched along one pale, straw-papered wall.

She watched as he filled first her glass then his own, and placed the bottle on the table between them before seating himself opposite her.

'Happy reunions!' he said softy and succinctly, raising his glass, motioning it towards her before lifting it to his lips and taking a long draught.

Nella shrugged. 'Why not?' The wine was full-bodied and long in flavour. She recognised both its quality and its potency, savouring it on her palate, knowing that her capacity to imbibe it and keep her sense about her was strictly limited.

She watched as Raúl sliced into his steak. Dark on the outside, it pinkened towards the centre. The serrated knife had cleaved through it without difficulty, and if the efficacy of his teeth was in line with their undoubted pulchritude her feral companion should have little difficulty in consuming it.

His small nod of appreciation confirmed her opinion, and despite the irritability of her feelings towards him Nella found herself relaxing.

'I wasn't sure how you would like it cooked,' she said, finding the silence slightly oppressive. 'I seem to remember reading somewhere that Americans prefer their steaks well-done.'

'Which is why you left the middle raw?' he murmured ironically, slanting her a quizzical smile. 'Your cooking is obviously better than your geography. Venezuela is not part of the United States of America.'

'Well, of course I know that...' she started huffily, wondering what had inspired her to make the allusion in the first place.

'What else do you know about my country?'

It was a direct challenge and one she forced herself to meet, searching into the hidden files of her memory for inspiration. 'It's a democracy on the north coast of South America, capital Caracas. The main river is the Orinoco, its wealth is based on oil...'

'Excellent!' Raúl nodded his dark head approvingly. 'Luis has been a diligent teacher. I assume he told you that his purpose in the UK was to persuade your travel agencies to promote package holidays in Venezuela?'

'Actually, he didn't——'

He didn't allow her to finish her sentence, but swept on regardless of her frustrated frown. 'Not too strenuous an undertaking, even for a young and comparatively inexperienced salesman, since we enjoy a Caribbean coastline which rivals those of the islands, an interior which is wild and beautiful, the highest waterfall in the world——'

'The Angel Falls,' Nella interposed succinctly, determined not to be dismissed as a moron. 'I've always thought how fortunate it was that the pilot who discovered them by accident just happened to be named Angel. Just think if they'd been found by—by—Joshua Ramsbottom, for example.' She smiled into the glowing red depths of her wine-glass, inhaling the aroma before taking a long, sweet swallow. 'Not that there's anything wrong with the name Ramsbottom,' she hastened to add, observing the slightly raised eyebrows of her companion. 'Just that since the falls are so high that they appear to be coming from heaven the name "Angel" is particularly apt.'

Raúl brushed aside her gabbling with the derision it no doubt deserved.

'Is that how you trapped Luis into marrying you?' he enquired, pushing away his plate before placing his elbows on the table and resting his granite-hewn chin on the back of his elevated hands. 'By swotting up on your geography and pretending to share his patriotic enthusiasm for his homeland?' Bitterness edged the soft timbre of his voice. 'Why couldn't you have been content with just accepting his gifts, Nella? God knows, he's always been generous to a fault with his lovers. What did he do to you to make you hate him so much that you had no qualms about going through the farce of marriage in order to bankrupt him financially as well as emotionally?'

'Nothing! He did nothing...' Furiously Nella propelled herself upward in her seat, pushing it away from her, her cheeks flushed from the wine and frustration. She knew that it was pointless to reiterate her innocence, and was intent on finding sanctuary away from her tormentor, having learned from experience that when reason was ineffective, there was no humiliation in retreat. It was often the simplest and kindest course of action to take for all concerned.

'Not so fast, my lovely!' Raúl sprang to his feet barring her exit.

'You expect me stay here and listen to your insults?' Her chin tilted at a disdainful angle.

'If I wish it, yes.' His voice was measured, yet contained an undertone of cold contempt as he made no attempt to allow her free passage. 'But my opinion of you is not totally without respect. I admit a grudging admiration for the way you went about your task to defraud, and the way you selected your victim. Luis was a foreigner, gullible and hot-blooded, and his time in England was limited. You would have observed from his clothes and from his generosity that he was not a poor man. Perhaps you thought he was rich enough to be able to sustain such a loss as you intended inflicting on him without complaint? That he'd do so willingly rather than confess he'd been the humiliated victim of a confidence trick? That he'd have neither the time nor the inclination to pursue you and avenge himself, hmm?'

A strong hand rose to imprison her upper arm, fingers tightening like a steel hawser round the tender pale flesh exposed by the sleeveless blouse as he posed his question with a vulpine sneer. 'If you believed he could afford to lose twenty thousand pounds without flinching, *querida*, then you selected the wrong brother as your victim...'

'But then, of course, at the time I devised my dastardly and intricate plan I hadn't had the pleasure of making *your* acquaintance, had I?' Nella enquired sweetly, all thought of making a dignified retreat now obliterated from her mind. For pity's sake—Raúl wasn't mentally impaired, was he? Just bull-headed and bigoted and not worthy of her respect in the way that Rosie had been!

'Pleasure?' His scorching regard seared her contentiously raised face, causing her pulse to quicken as it responded to the adrenalin charge of embryonic fear which tautened every nerve of her body. 'Yes, Nella, you're right. It *would* have been a pleasure for you, in ways you probably can't even imagine.' Slowly, impertinently, his beautiful eyes took a toll of her body, as if her clothes had suddenly become invisible. 'For me, too, the experience would doubtless have been an enjoyable one. An expert ensemble always gives a more satisfying performance than an amateur one, no? But there would have been one difference. When it was over *you* would have been the abandoned one—used and robbed.'

Heat flooded her body, rising in a wave which brought a flush of colour to her cheeks, allied to an unexpected determination not to be cowed by Raúl's scorn. Forced to control her responses in the face of false accusations from Rosie in the past, now it was as if the cruel lash of his tongue had sliced through her practised reserve, to destroy the dam of restraint she'd erected. In that instant she forgot that it was some other woman to whom he was referring, some woman who deserved to be the recipient of his disgust.

'Don't flatter yourself, Raúl.' A stifling sensation caught at her throat as his eyes remained fixed unwaveringly on her face, but she forced herself to continue. 'Hasn't any woman dared to tell you that the myth of the macho brute's desirability has been exploded? That charm and gentleness in the male species has come back into fashion?'

The narrow smile he offered her was totally without humour. 'Don't deceive yourself, Nella. The only reason you might have thought twice about taking me on is that your cunning little mind might have warned you that you didn't stand a chance in hell of manipulating and cheating me. I'm too clever for you. I would have thought that fact was obvious by now.'

'You mean because you tracked me down to David's house?' Her breath was ragged and her heart seemed to have discovered a beat not too distant from that of the calypso rhythm, but she held her ground, assuming a nonchalance she was far from feeling. 'Yes, how did you manage that?'

'I went to Seabeach Holiday Camp, of course. When Luis made his rapturous and defiant phone call, informing me of his newly married state, he made no secret of your Cinderella past. Fortunately, a taped copy was automatically made, as is the case with all intercontinental calls I take.' His mouth shadowed with a self-mocking smile. 'My country has many attributes of which I am justly proud. Unfortunately, the fast and efficient delivery of inter-continental mail is not one of them. Luis chose to break his news by phone rather than over the more public facility of the office fax machine. It was a long call. He was already feeling the first twinges of apprehension about his foolhardy gesture and was anxious to win me over, to persuade me to smooth his path so that when he returned to Caracas with his wife she would be made welcome.'

'And did you agree?' she challenged curiously.

'No.' A shadow of pain seemed to dull the brightness of his eyes for a fleeting instant, as if he regretted his adamantine decision. 'I refused to take any action until I'd met you and formed my own judgement about your suitability to become a member of our family. I told him I would come over to England as soon as business permitted, and that until then I intended to keep the news to myself.' He paused slightly, then asked, 'You knew nothing of this call?'

Nella sighed. 'Not a thing,' she admitted honestly. 'Did he normally ask you to fight his battles for him?'

'Inevitably.' He shrugged his shoulders wearily. 'In this instance my response was quicker than intended. Two days before I was due to leave Caracas I was contacted and informed of Luis's accident. I left immediately.'

'Went to his apartment——'

'And discovered the whole fradulent story!' His mouth snapped shut in a grim line. 'After visiting Luis, and the registrar, I made Seabeach my first call.'

'And they gave you David's address?' His means of tracing her to Devon had been a nagging problem at the back of her mind.

He nodded. 'After I proved to them that I was your brother-in-law and had urgent need to contact you. Easy, wasn't it—even for Luis? Why else do you suppose that it was just outside Exeter that, tired, stressed and emotionally exhausted, Luis crashed his car?'

He lifted a forefinger to caress the exposed skin of Nella's arm, and it quivered beneath his hand as he con-

tinued in an even voice, 'Not only were you careless in
leaving a trail, but you underestimated the extent of his
pride. Luis's head may rule his heart but he would allow
no one to impugn his honour. You made a bad mistake
in naming your brother as your next of kin on your personnel file. How bad, you have yet to discover.'

'I realise that now!' It was no more than the truth,
although Nella had no doubts that it would be received
as an admission of her guilt. If only David had been in
a less vulnerable position, she would have told Raúl
Farrington exactly what he could have done with his
forged marriage certificate! 'Unfortunately, since my
grandmother's death two years ago, he's the only relative
I have.'

'And he has no time for you, hmm?' His narrowed
eyes probed her reserve with their edged brilliance.
'David Lambert, MP-to-be, didn't want to be saddled
with the little scrubber who was his sister, hmm?'

'That's not true!' she flashed, hiding hurt with a show
of anger. David *did* care for her! It was just that they'd
shared so little of their lives, through circumstances not
of their making, that they were almost strangers. It was
true she'd taken the full brunt of Rosie's dreadful illness,
but then that was only to be expected. Her lips twisted
wryly. It wasn't only in the Latin 'macho' societies that
women were considered to be the 'carers'. Besides, Rosie
had devoted herself to looking after her when her mother
had emigrated to Australia without a backward look,
and David had been generous in his financial support.
And when her grandmother had finally died, and left
her Cambridgeshire house to be divided between her two
grandchildren, it had been David who had taken on the
full responsibility of handling the sale, so she had been
free to escape to the saner, gentler world of Seabeach.

'Isn't it?' Raúl's piercing blue eyes burned into her wide-eyed amber gaze. 'He didn't seem overly distressed at your leaving the party.'

'Because he knew I wouldn't have gone without a good reason.' She tried to shake herself free of his hold. 'How do you know about his standing at the by-election, anyway?'

'Because I made full enquiries about him and his family before going to the house. For all I knew he might have been your accomplice in fleecing Luis.' He ignored her sigh of exasperation. 'When I discovered that it was the first time you'd visited him for several years, I realised he was just another victim of your self-interest.'

Nella's eyes flashed formidably at Raúl's smug expression. 'I happen to care deeply for my brother.'

'Indeed, that's what I'm counting on, *querida*.' His soft answer held a menacing echo in its deep timbre. 'And now you have another brother to love as well, no?' His firm mouth twisted into a malicious smile. 'Tomorrow when we visit Luis in hospital he will be overjoyed to see us together.' It wasn't something she'd bet on! Nella thought waspishly. Poor Luis, he was in for a dreadful shock when Raúl produced her. A deep wave of pity drenched her heart as she pictured the mental and physical anguish of the young Venezuelan confined to his hospital bed.

'How badly hurt is he?' She gazed directly into Raúl's clear, angry eyes, ashamed that she'd been too caught up with her own problems not to have asked the question earlier.

'He'll survive—unfortunately for you.' His nostrils flared as if he'd scented her innate apprehension about the meeting ahead. 'So if you had any ideas of becoming a wealthy widow—forget them!' His cold gaze raked over her, transfixing her in its power, as the tension which primed every golden inch of his smooth, tough skin bridged the gap between their bodies—a phenomenon which left her shaken and trembling, silent in the face of the bitterness which etched cruel lines on his personable face.

'Why couldn't you have been content with just his heart, Nella?' His other hand came up to imprison her jaw, lean fingers following the slender oval bones, one drifting away to trace the soft full curves of her pink mouth with a menacing gentleness. 'Why did you have to steal the money in his custody, and with it his honour and nearly his life as well?' Bleak and deadly, his question assaulted her ears. 'Did you really believe you'd be allowed to get away with it?'

'Whatever I did, whatever I believed—it's between Luis and me.' His jagged censure drove her to find a stance she could defend as she pulled herself free from his contemptuous caress, alarmed by the dark emotion which seemed to swirl around him, reaching out tenuous fingers to envelop her. 'Perhaps if you'd interfered less with his affairs in the past he would have been less easily duped?'

Panting and dishevelled by her successful efforts to escape his hold she remained facing him, arms crossed, each hand clasping its opposite shoulder defensively as she tried to control the tremors which racked her body.

'Finish your meal, Nella.' To her intense relief he moved away from her, back to the table, and poured himself another glass of wine.

'You mean the inquisition's over?' she asked in disbelief.

'I mean I accept your argument as valid.' He regarded her with studied insolence. 'Another man might attempt to beat the truth out of you but, as you have pointed out to me, your chastisement is not my prerogative.' He sipped his wine thoughtfully as she glared at him belligerently. 'I shall have to hope that Luis's recent experience has toughened him enough to deal with you. In the meantime there seems little purpose in prolonging this shouting-match.'

'Precisely.' Nella capitulated rather than exacerbate the situation, retracing her steps to the table and settling down in front of the remains of her meal, conscious that her appetite had waned considerably since their angry altercation. 'Although why you couldn't take me to Luis this evening is beyond me. Surely hospital rules don't preclude a wife from seeing a husband outside normal visiting hours in the case of an accident?'

'Luis is still very tired after his ordeal. He sleeps a great deal.' A slight shrug accompanied the explanation. 'Hopefully, after another good night's sleep, he'll be more prepared for your reunion.'

He took a mouthful of steak, masticating it with closed mouth as his eyes devoured her face, absorbing her air of weary frustration, and swallowing before speaking again. 'Tell me, Nella,' he asked conversationally, 'what have you done with the money you stole? Buried it under your brother's floorboards, or rebanked it in your maiden name?'

Nella flinched. How stupid she'd been in believing Raúl had truly intended to cease his cross-examination. It wasn't the first time she'd been wrongly and consistently accused of misbehaving, but the injustice still stung with the rawness of acid. As her grandmother's condition had deteriorated the old lady had consistently accused her of stealing her jewellery and selling her clothes. Clothes she'd long since discarded; jewellery which she'd never possessed. At first she'd denied the charges angrily, then she'd realised it was impossible to reason with something suffering from dementia. And because Rosie had loved and nurtured her as a child, and she returned her affection, she'd gone along with her, not denying or accepting the accusations but promising that tomorrow everything would be replaced. And as, in Rosie's world, tomorrow never came, the promise of reparation was always new, always soothing to her troubled mind and welcomed.

But there was nothing wrong with Raúl Farrington's mind. No reason why she should humour him. 'Neither of those things,' she told him coldly. 'And frankly, if Luis was prepared to make such a large sum of someone else's money available to a woman he'd just met, then he was asking for trouble.'

Her breath seemed to burn in her throat as Raúl's face froze into a mask of controlled fury. She'd already gone too far, a little further would make no difference to the strength of the wrath about to descend on her head, and she was experiencing an unexpected excitement in partaking in this duel of words. Like a prisoner who was offered the prospect of running cross-country after being incarcerated for years in a narrow cell.

'But then from what I've observed about you to date, intelligence appears to take a lesser place to uninformed bluster in the characteristics of the Farrington family,' she ended triumphantly.

There was a moment's deathly silence before Raúl rose to his feet. 'Then inform me, *guapa*,' he commanded insolently, gripping the edge of the table with both hands as if he was about to tip it and its contents over the dark-stained floorboards.

Nella was trembling, all the bottled up tension of the past years shaken and regurgitating in her mind, just when she thought she'd returned to a life of peace and sanity. A small, quiet portion of her reason sympathised with Raúl's predicament, his deep and genuine worry for his brother's health, his equally deep concern that Luis should not face a criminal charge, but a greater part demanded she should defend herself against injustice. All she had asked for was time. Time would resolve the first part of her problem. More time would undoubtedly resolve the deeper part of the mystery as to why someone had filched her identity. Time was not what Raúl Farrington was prepared to give her.

She jumped to her feet, determined to meet him on the same level, her eyes blazing, her hair a shimmering mass of red-gold on the cream satin shoulders of her blouse. 'No—why should I? You haven't listened to a word I've been saying since the moment you stormed into my life. As far as I'm concerned you can get all the information you need from Luis tomorrow. Until then I've got nothing to say.' A tremor of alarm at her own daring trembled down her spine as she perceived the glint in his eyes which signalled that the time had come when it would be in her own interests to show a little discretion. Restraining her sharper impulses, she added civilly, 'Now, if you've finished your meal, I'd better get on with the washing-up.'

'Leave it.' His instruction was brief. Did it even contain a brief echo of respect for her stand? Surely not? she thought, confused. Yet something told her that Raúl Farrington would acknowledge bravery—even in an enemy. 'I'll see to it,' he continued abruptly, perplexing her further, before adding, 'You'll need a good night's sleep before coming face to face with the man you deceived.'

There was no mercy in the direct gaze he turned on her. He wanted her fresh for the kill, was already anticipating the joys of seeing her twisting and turning to escape when confronted with the man he believed she'd treated so appallingly.

'The prospect of that would have been enhanced if you'd informed me at the start that I should be prepared for an overnight stay,' she flung at him.

'Possibly,' he snapped back at her. 'But I wanted to take you while the element of surprise was still alive.'

His light eyes dwelt lingeringly on her camellia-like skin, an unusual fire glimmering in their shining depths as, to her horror, Nella felt a warm tide of sensation surge through every cell of her body. Immediately and shamefully she found herself recalling his touch, his taste, his scent as he'd given her that brutal punitive kiss outside the cottage, imprinting his mark on her as surely and indelibly as a security pen on a valued piece of property. The words 'I wanted to take you...' bounced off the walls of her mind like ping-pong balls at a tournament.

He was the first to regain his power of speech. 'However,' he added calmly, 'I am not entirely without *hidalguia*. Charlatan though you undoubtedly are, it is not part of your penalty that you should sleep naked in bed, or wear unlaundered lingerie, or be deprived of the luxury of modern toilette aids. You will find everything you need in the bedroom at the back of the house.'

'Your generosity astounds me, Raúl.' She curled her tongue round his name, liking the feel of it, as she cast

him a sardonic smile, more certain of her ground now
she'd been dismissed.

'Then make the most of it, Nella,' he growled, unsmiling. 'Because from now on you will find it in
little evidence.'

# CHAPTER FOUR

WHAT did her domineering captor consider to be adequate luxury for a woman he believed should be serving a term in prison? Nella wondered morosely, pushing open the door to the back bedroom half expecting to find a flannel nightdress, a toothbrush and a bar of carbolic soap supplied for her use.

Entering, she found herself blinking as the centre light sprang into life at her touch on the switch, illuminating a room which was pretty rather than elegant. Chintz curtains hung at the windows, their main colour echoing the rose-pink of the fitted carpet, plain white built-in cupboards surrounded a large mirror above a fitted dressing-table and the full-sized bed behind the open door was strewn with a paler pink duvet. But then the imperious Venezuelan had had no hand in choosing the décor.

It was what was on the duvet which drew a breath of astonishment from her mouth. The nightdress was of the palest *eau-de-Nil*, the material a thick slippery satin, the style simple. Holding it up to admire it more closely, Nella observed that it was little more than a beautifully tailored sleeveless sheath, with a deep V-neck, front and back, and the skirt an inverted tulip-shape, which would cling to the hips but flare around the ankles.

It came with its own cover-up, a matching full-length kimono-style coat in the same fabric with an embroidered sash. On the floor she espied a pair of satin mules, and couldn't resist slipping a foot out of its shoe to try one on. Half a size too large—but wearable!

Turning her head, she gazed at the array of bottles and jars which lined the top of the dressing-table. Deodorant, talcum, moisturiser, hand-cream and an assortment of make-up as well as the more mundane soap, flannel and towels. Even perfume! Bemused, she approached nearer, to find what Raúl had selected for her to scent herself with. Something musky and provocative, suitable for the scarlet woman he supposed her to be? Picking up the boxed atomiser, she shook her head in bewilderment. Contrary to expectation, he had chosen one of her very favourite perfumes—light and elusive, fragrant yet fresh.

Her mouth curved in a rueful smile. Raúl was obviously ensuring she smelt the way he liked women to smell rather than the way he guessed, incorrectly, that she would have chosen.

Curiosity getting the better of her as she recalled his mention of lingerie, Nella pulled open the top drawer of the chest of drawers and found herself staring at a transparent pack bearing a famous lingerie manufacturer's name. Quickly she tore the packaging and slid the contents into her hands, a wry smile turning her lips as she gazed at an ecru-coloured camisole top and matching French knickers. Even Raúl Farrington hadn't dared to presume to guess the size of bra she wore! Both garments had been chosen in a size specified as 'medium'.

Apparently, Luis's descriptions of his wife had managed to convey her general stature without being too intimately specific about her precise measurements. How fortunate that the younger Farrington brother hadn't fallen in love with a five feet two matchstick of a girl! She fingered the ecru silk thoughtfully. Whoever had decided to take her name and identity must look very much like her—similar type of figure, similar colouring. Obviously the fact that the two of them bore a surface resemblance must have motivated her impersonator in the first place. But she knew no one who remotely resembled her!

She thrust the niggling problem out of her mind. Tomorrow. She must be patient, because tomorrow, if it did not provide a solution to the riddle, would at least put her in the clear as far as her irate captor was concerned, and remove any threat of damage to David's ambitions. Of course, the bizarre situation would have to be investigated and corrected, but once her total uninvolvement in the masquerade had been determined, it could be done discreetly.

There was no movement from downstairs as she entered the bathroom to take a quick shower, enjoying the fragrance of the luxurious body-gel provided. Afterwards she briskly towelled herself dry before donning the nightdress and wrap and flitting rapidly across the landing to the sanctuary of her room, her day-clothes over her arm. Fortunately the trousers and blouse had been worn for only a short period, and if placed carefully on a hanger overnight would pass muster the next day.

Wearily she climbed into the bed, relaxing in its soft yet resilient comfort. To her customary brief and silent prayers she added the name of Luis Farrington, asking that he would be granted a swift recovery from his injuries and fortitude to bear the calamity which had overtaken him.

She awakened to birdsong and a wall of gently moving flowers as sunshine filtering through the chintz curtains and a breeze from the open window brought the perfume of roses into the room. Thank heavens Raúl's precautions for securely confining her hadn't included locking her bedroom window! Presumably he considered that even she, wickedly motivated as he supposed her to be, would have difficulty in squeezing through such a small space several feet from the ground!

A sharp rap at her door had her grabbing the duvet up to her neck, conscious of the expanse of pale cleavage exposed by the dipped neckline of the nightdress.

'Yes?'

She'd meant the word merely as an enquiry, but Raúl took it as an invitation to enter. He came in carrying a small tray bearing a steaming cup of fragrant coffee, a small milk jug and sugar bowl and a china plate bearing two croissants which, from their deliciously appetising aroma, appeared to have been newly baked.

'I thought as you cooked the dinner I should be responsible for breakfast,' he informed her gravely, lifting a white linen table-napkin from the tray and placing it over her lap before covering it with the tray. 'I regret I'm not conversant with cooking an English breakfast, so you'll have to make do with a continental one.'

'Thank you,' Nella said faintly, her eyes travelling swiftly over him from head to foot, assessing what was a vision of exquisitely groomed vibrant manhood in its prime. From the hips down, pale grey trousers followed the line of long, hard-muscled thighs and hinted at equally solid and shapely calves. Above the thin leather belt which graced the dropped waistline there stretched a short-sleeved round-necked cotton T-shirt the same breathtaking colour as his eyes. A pale sea of colour against the light, tanned column of his throat, it outlined exercise-tuned pectorals and demonstrated in the simplest way possible that not one ounce of excess fat or muscle marred the perfectly toned structure of his waist and stomach.

'I take it you approve?' The soft question with its hint of underlying amusement was enough to make the blood rush to Nella's cheeks. What on earth had she been doing, anyway?

Knowing there would be no pleasure for her in making love without being in love, her relationships at college had always been platonic. Even the closeness she'd felt with Michael, the young doctor who'd supervised Rosie's treatment, had been based on gratitude for his support, and she'd been wise enough to turn down his proposal of marriage after Rosie's funeral, knowing he deserved a wife who would really love him.

Now she found the strange feelings which were flooding her body painful and unwelcome—no, more than that, *humiliating*, in view of his insolent attitude towards her and the certainty that not only would he be married but sire of a small brood of equally impossible Farringtons!

'I'm referring to the breakfast, *querida*.' He stepped away from her, regarding her with a look of assumed innocence which sat strangely on a face seasoned with experience and incident. 'The coffee is pure Colombian, the croissants freshly baked.'

'So I supposed.' With an effort Nella regained her composure. Tossing her head in an effort to free a lock of hair which had curled into the back of her neck, she succeeded in making her full mane of fine Titian hair swirl about her shoulders. Lifting one hand to steady the tray on her lap, she was unaware of the duvet slipping to reveal the pure perfection of her pale shoulders, the fine, sensitive skin unmarked by the sun.

Some fleeting expression which blazed in Raúl's clear eyes warned her that unknowingly she was courting danger. Afraid that her reply had sounded too pert, and anxious to retain some semblance of courtesy between them, she added swiftly, 'I had no idea you were an expert baker.'

'I'm not,' he drawled, denying the suggestion with a faint supercilious lift of the corners of his mouth. 'As I'm sure Luis must have told you, my expertise lies more in directing others what to do rather than doing it myself. But when I came down here to check over the cottage I noticed a bakery in a nearby village which was advertising the availability of freshly baked rolls every morning from eight o'clock onwards.'

'Your brother never discussed you with me at all.' Nella offered him a saccharine-sweet smile as, disregarding the milk and sugar, she took a long, refreshing draught of fragrant coffee. 'Mmm, delicious,' she said approvingly, adding brightly in an effort to defuse the electrical energy which she sensed arcing between them, 'Are croissants normal breakfast fare in Caracas?'

'For those who like them. I prefer *arepas*.' Then, seeing her questioning look, 'They're a speciality of my country—cornflour pancakes crisp on the outside and incredibly soft on the inside. They make excellent snacks too, when they're filled with meat and vegetables. It may not be too long before you have the opportunity of trying them.'

The timbre of his voice made the possibility sound like a threat, and acted as a sinister warning of the plans he must be making. Unable to resist the challenge, now she was so close to being vindicated, Nella decided she could afford to bait him a little.

'You intend to take me back to Caracas?' she asked, deliberately keeping her voice free of emotion. Despite the comforting knowledge that he had no jurisdiction over her movements whatsoever, she felt apprehensive, like a small child offering a morsel of food to a large dog, uncertain whether she would get her hand bitten off for her trouble—or, in her case, her head!

Raúl's speculative gaze drifted slowly over the revealed portions of her body. Knowing her question had unwittingly invited his inspection, she forced herself not to flinch beneath that excoriating appraisal, but was helpless to prevent the pale flush of colour which pinkened the exposed alabaster skin covering the swell of her breasts. As a matter of pride she forced herself to keep her head high and the lips of her soft mouth tightly closed as her hazel eyes remained pinned to the almost Aztec beauty of his facial bones.

'An interesting question,' he purred at last. 'And one to which I cannot yet give a definite answer. My first impulse on learning of your deceit was to insist on a divorce, since your motives for entering into the union were totally venal. However, you are not the first woman to marry in order to get your hands on a man's money— although the majority of your sisters do not reveal their cupidity so early in the relationship.' His lips twisted, and a flicker of irony lit in the depths of his eyes as they assessed the challenging expression on her face. 'Now I'm beginning to think a better solution would be for you to accompany Luis back to Caracas and learn the ways of a *caraqueña*. It could prove a salutary lesson to both of you.'

'So Luis has no say in the matter?' Nella demanded, deciding not to enter a debate on divorce procedure in the English courts.

He shrugged off her question with a disdainful movement of his broad shoulders. 'I should think that Luis is no longer so confident in his ability to make personal decisions, wouldn't you?' The question was purely rhetorical as he went on, with barely an interval for breath, 'I anticipate he'll take my advice on the matter.'

'And you believe your sister-in-law will be as complaisant?' Nella enquired in dulcet tones. 'Suppose she doesn't fancy emigrating?'

The quick flash of Raúl's teeth, as his firm lips parted in a half-smile, half-snarl, warned her that she wouldn't like his reply!

'In that case you should have used your charms on a rich Englishman. Because if you do decide to stay here in opposition to Luis's wishes, I'll see you're publicly stripped of every claim to virtue and respectability. I'll ensure that the tabloid newspapers receive full details of your heartless trickery and that the name Lambert becomes a synonym for deception and fraud. Does that answer your question satisfactorily?' His eyes rested on her, alive with contentious speculation, tempting her to combat.

Nella shivered. There was no future for her in provoking him further. She was trapped in the no-man's-land of being unable to prove her innocence and, frustrating though such a position was, it was better than provoking Raúl Farrington beyond the point where he was able to control his baser instincts.

Instead, she forced herself to offer him a small, placatory smile. 'A very succinct exposition,' she agreed, then, as she saw his brows meet in a puzzled frown, she took advantage of his silence to ask, 'What time did you go out for the rolls? I didn't hear the car start up.'

'Because I didn't take it,' he retorted calmly. 'I decided to walk and experience the English countryside at first hand. I found it fresh and beautiful, simple on the surface but almost certainly full of hidden promises and delights. During Luis's convalescence you must introduce me more fully to everything it can offer.'

She must have been imagining things, because she thought she'd detected a current of challenge underlying the overt smoothness of his suggestion, and the way he was looking at her, his dark brows lowered over narrowed, perceptive eyes, did nothing to comfort her. Quickly she pursued another track.

'What's the time?'

'Nine o'clock.'

'That late?' She broke a portion of sweetly scented croissant and placed it on her tongue, where it all but melted. 'I never lie in that long!'

'The Cabernet Sauvignon must have calmed your conscience,' he suggested smoothly. 'I left quietly so as not to disturb you, having no wish to deprive you of your beauty sleep. You will wish to look your best for this morning's reunion with your husband.'

Deliberately Nella refrained from looking at him or reacting to his latest comment, contenting herself with enjoying the breakfast he'd provided for her.

'Just in case you wondered,' he continued conversationally, with a lilt in his voice which suggested suppressed amusement, 'I took the precaution of deadlocking all the doors and downstairs windows when I went out. I should have hated to have returned and found my nest empty.'

'You wasted your time and energy,' Nella informed him coolly, swallowing the last crumb before taking a final mouthful of coffee. 'Believe me, Raúl, nothing is going to give me greater pleasure than meeting Luis face-to-face this morning!' She raised her beautiful hazel eyes to meet his personable face, dismissing him with a quiet dignity. 'I'd be obliged if you'd take this tray away and leave my bedroom. The breakfast was delicious and the conversation accompanying it—riveting. Now I'd like time and privacy to get myself ready for our visit to the hospital.'

The raven head dipped in silent acquiescence as Raúl took the proferred tray from her hands and moved toward the door. She kept her eyes fastened on his back, absorbing the proud carriage of his head, the movement of the deltoid muscles as he reached for the door-handle, the way the light, summer-weight material of his trousers hugged the taut lines of his hips with their hollowed loins and tight male buttocks. Only when the door closed behind him and she was alone did she expel her pent-up breath in one long drawn-out sigh.

Her pulse was racing, her skin beneath its pale silk covering was damp, and the odd fluttering she felt in the region of her stomach, she accepted with a spasm of dismay, had nothing to do with the croissants and coffee which she'd just consumed.

Two hours later, after a brief introduction to the ward sister, Nella found herself standing mutely beside Raúl as he enquired about his brother's condition. Feeling faint from a mixture of emotions as she anticipated the imminent trauma about to inflict itself on everyone concerned within the next few minutes, she took no exception to Raúl's firm hold beneath her right elbow. There would be a deep satisfaction in watching her companion's face as Luis denied all knowledge of her, but her heart ached for the younger man. Did he still love the false Nella? she wondered, shifting her weight slightly from one leg to the other.

She felt uncomfortable. Not just because of the forth-coming ordeal but because, unused to going without a bra, she was finding the continuous rub of the camisole top against her nipples oddly disturbing. Likewise, the French knickers, while undoubtedly glamorous, moved seductively against her thighs as she walked and felt de-cidedly strange in place of the plain cotton briefs she normally wore. At least, she mused, she could be grateful that she hadn't decided to wear jeans. Thankfully her trousers were styled to accommodate, without be-traying, the more fanciful type of underwear with which she'd been provided. A tremor shivered down her back. How grateful she was to know that Raúl's predatory fingers had never touched the ecru silk which she was finding so distracting.

'Satisfactory,' the sister was saying. She was young and attractive, her blonde hair short and curly beneath her tiny frilled cap. 'It's impossible to say exactly when he'll come completely out of his coma, but the signs are very positive. As you know, he's already experienced a few waking moments. He knows he's had an accident and that he's in hospital. He's also spoken a few dis-jointed words.' She smiled at Nella. 'In particular your name, Mrs Farrington. It's not unusual for patients to experience deep trauma after an accident like this, but it's possible that your presence will be all that is necessary to bring him back to full consciousness. Shall we see?'

Coma? Nella went rigid, her mind stunned by shock. Luis Farrington was in a coma? All these hours she'd been consoling herself with the thought that this absurd misidentification would be acknowledged, and now she was about to be taken to the bedside of an unconscious man!

'Wait, please!' She swallowed the lump in her throat with an effort, her sharp tone halting the sister in mid-stride. 'You mean Mr Farrington is concussed?'

'You didn't know?' A slight frown creased the other woman's forehead. 'I thought your brother-in-law would have told you...' Her quick glance went from one face to the other.

'I didn't want to worry Nella unduly,' Raúl explained smoothly. 'I was hoping that after four days there might have been some improvement.'

'I see.' The Sister accepted his explanation with a sympathetic smile before turning to Nella. 'Your husband has a broken arm, which naturally has been set, and extensive bruising to his ribcage and abdomen caused by the restraint of his seatbelt. He also suffered mild concussion, but, as I told your brother-in-law, the prognosis is good, although of course we have been monitoring his condition regularly in case of internal haemorrhage.'

'But mild concussion...' Nella protested desperately. 'Shouldn't that have improved by now?'

'I'm afraid there are no hard and fast rules with the brain, Mrs Farrington,' the blonde woman said placatingly. 'There may be psychological factors involved which are delaying his early return to full consciousness.'

If she but knew! Trapped into silence, Nella nodded her carefully coiffed head in acceptance of the diagnosis. In deference to the heatwave which was holding the country in its thrall, she had brushed her wealth of hair to the top of her head before plaiting it into a tail which ran from crown to nape, secured in a small coil at her lower hairline. The only problem was that it was a style which exposed her face cruelly and entirely to Raúl's critical appraisal, robbing her of the benefit of subterfuge.

'Shocked, *querida*?' he whispered against her ear as the sister led the way to a room outside the main ward. 'Don't tell me you have any real feelings for my brother? Or is it that you're afraid you'll have an invalid on your hands in the near future?'

Still reeling from the way fate had treated her, Nella forbore to answer, as Raúl's fingers tightened ruthlessly around her upper arm. 'Don't worry, Nella. The Farringtons have strong bones and hard heads as well as a lusty desire to avenge themselves on those who wrong them. Once Luis hears the sound of your voice, he will regain consciousness. I'm depending on it!'

So was she. Nella's spine stiffened, but she held her tongue.

The sister opened the door and stood back, beckoning the nurse who was seated at Luis's bedside to leave the room before closing it quietly behind them. As she moved slowly towards the solitary bed and gazed down at its occupant, a wave of compassion swept over Nella.

Luis Farrington lay as if asleep, one arm connected to a drip, the other encased in plaster. Blue-black hair, straighter and longer than Raúl's, was a dramatic blot of colour on the white pillow. His face was still, beautiful in repose, the long dark lashes fanned on his cheek, his breathing steady. There was only a cursory likeness between the brothers, she thought, staring down at him, not far from tears as her gentle heart responded to his suffering. There was none of the predatory hawk in Luis's less aggressive features, and his bones were less finely chiselled. Only the mouth was redolent of Raúl's, with its sweet, sweeping curves, the equally balanced broadness of the well-formed lips.

Raúl stood somewhere behind her, between her and the door, but Nella had no thought of flight. Moving slowly, driven by an impulse based on pure compassion, she moved to seat herself on the edge of the bed, taking the cold fingers of the splinted arm into her own.

'Oh, Luis,' she murmured, lifting her free hand to brush the dark hair away from his forehead. 'What have you done to yourself?'

He was her own age, she remembered, dipping her head to lay her warm cheek against the still fingers, as if to instil some life into them. But, unlike her, he must be impetuous and volatile—how else could he have married a woman he had scarcely known? And, worse than that, given her access to money which hadn't been his in the first place? Silly, infatuated young man...

A qualm of disquiet stirred somewhere inside her. As the sister had said, the brain was a law unto itself, subject to many influences. Suppose that Luis had been so distraught by what had befallen him that he had no wish to regain consciousness and face the consequences? Or suppose he regained consciousness but his memory deliberately blotted out all knowledge of the woman he had married? A small pulse began to beat agitatedly in her throat.

'Speak to him, damn you!'

Behind her, Raúl's voice grated the instruction, 'Say his name. Tell him you're sorry for the way you behaved, that you've come back to him and brought the money you took with you.'

'No!' Nella's head rose with the speed of a cobra about to strike as she grasped the yawning pit opening before her. 'No! I can't do that!'

'You can, and you will.' Like shards of ice Raúl's voice stung her ears. 'Or your beloved brother can kiss goodbye to being elected! Lie, sweetheart. You managed it before. See how much better you can do it when the prize is keeping your name and that of your family out of the gutter press.'

'Raúl, please!' She jumped to her feet. 'It's impossible——'

How to explain to him that her reticence was on her brother's behalf, that she'd be doing him no favour by lying?

Oblivious to her agony, Raúl moved behind her to take one arm in a fierce grasp, ignoring her gasp of discomfort.

'Tell him, Nella,' he instructed her, each word razor-sharp. 'Tell him, or I won't be responsible for the consequences.'

It wasn't the implicit threat of a bruised arm which decided her, but rather the sudden convulsive movement of the young man in the bed. It had been his brother's voice which had broken into his dream world, not hers. Luis Farrington had never heard her speak, but if there was the slightest chance that a woman's voice would stimulate his brain, then she knew she had to try!

'Luis,' she said hesitantly, then, gaining confidence, 'Luis, can you hear me? I've come to see you.'

The supine figure on the bed stirred, the eyelids fluttered and stilled.

'Tell him you're sorry!' Raúl's breath hissed in her ear.

'No!'

His grasp on her arm tightened. 'Tell him, *ramera*!'

Nella caught her breath in pain, as much at the cruel epithet of 'whore' as at the bite of his nails into her tender skin. Then, motivated more by Luis's movement than Raúl's bitter application, she did as she'd been instructed.

'I'm sorry Luis,' she cried out. 'I'm sorry you've been hurt. I'm sorry for everything that's happened to you!' She was breathing heavily, her gasps more redolent of sobs as the pathos of the situation struck hard at her heart. At least she was telling the truth—much good it would do either of them. 'Raúl,' she pleaded, twisting her head to stare into his adamantine face, 'this is going to get us nowhere!'

It was the face of an embittered angel which filled her vision, a terrifying beauty marred by lines of suffering. So Lucifer would have appeared in those first few moments of his expulsion from heaven. Flinching from the terrible pain reflected in the clear, shallow-sea-colour of his expressive eyes, Nella lapsed into silence.

On the bed Luis stirred, his dark head turning on the pillow, the fingers of his plastered arm scrabbling at the pristine cover, as if subconsciously he was aware of the tension building up in the small room.

'Once more,' Raúl instructed hardily. 'Tell him once more.'

She shook herself free, massaging the arm he'd maltreated, gathering her senses before walking back willingly to the side of the bed and dropping on her knees. She doubted many things, but one thing she had never doubted—that Raúl loved his brother and would stand by him through thick and thin, whatever his indiscretions. That knowledge helped her to find the right words. 'Luis—everything's going to be all right now,' she promised, closing her eyes and silently vowing that she would do her utmost to see that it was. 'Raúl and I will do everything in our power to help you.' Taking his hand, she raised it to her cheek.

Behind her she heard Raúl's quickly suppressed cry of triumph at the same time as the fingers moved against her cheek. Her eyes flared open to observe the flutter of Luis's eyelids. Lift and fall, lift and fall, until they lifted and hovered open, above eyes the colour of sun-ripened raisins.

She gasped and bit her lip, fearful of Luis's reaction as the dawn of intelligence illuminated his pale face and he drifted his gaze slowly over every line and hollow of her expectant, troubled face.

'Nella,' he whispered through parched lips. 'Nella—Raúl found you!'

# CHAPTER FIVE

IF SHE had been doused with a bucket of icy water Nella couldn't have felt more shocked and defeated, as her hopes of a speedy end to her ordeal splintered into fragments of despair to the accompaniment of Raúl's sharp exclamation of triumph.

'So much for your feeble lies.' The unbearable smugness of his tone made her cringe as she let Luis's nerveless hand fall to his side on the pristine cover, and turned in a last desperate effort to face her tormentor.

'He's still confused . . .' she began unhappily, keeping her voice low, unable to deny that the sparkle in the younger man's dark brown eyes had certainly betokened the presence of a familiar face, yet she knew without a doubt that she'd never set eyes on him in her life. 'Obviously the woman he married bore a resemblance to me——'

'A mirror image, doubtless,' he returned scornfully, his mouth hardening contemptuously before he returned his attention to his brother, whose eyelids had fluttered shut. Clasping Nella's upper arm, he drew her firmly to his side, insinuating his own formidable body between her and the young man in the bed.

'Don't worry, Luisito,' he exhorted softly, compassion thickening his tone as he gazed down at the supine figure. 'Now I've found her I have no intention of letting her escape. When you are well enough to deal with her be certain she will be ready and waiting to cooperate.'

What could she say? Too dazed by the unexpected demolition of the certainty that she had been about to be totally exonerated, Nella's mind spun in a maelstrom of horror as Luis's eyes flared open.

'No, Raúl, no!' Sweat stood out on the younger man's brow as he moved spasmodically, the words jerked from his lips with an obvious effort. 'Let her go... Send her away...' His head flailed on the pillow as he tried to raise one arm. 'I don't want her... She's not——' He broke off with a choked cry of pain as Raúl swore violently in Spanish, and, thrusting Nella from him, strode to the door yelling for medical assistance.

'What happened?' The sister was back in seconds, attending to the connection from the drip which had been pulled from Luis's hand in his efforts to speak, her eyes assessing her patient, who appeared to have lapsed back into unconsciousness.

'Over-excitement.' Raúl's expression was thunderous. 'I'm afraid my brother's reunion with his wife was more unsettling for him than I'd anticipated.'

'I see.' The nurse's glance roamed from Raúl's set face to Nella's blood-drained countenance. 'Perhaps it would be wiser if Mrs Farrington didn't visit again until her husband is a little stronger?' She cast Nella a sympathetic look. 'Try not to be too distressed, Mrs Farrington. Your husband has suffered a great deal of trauma. What he needs now is time to recuperate in a stress-free atmosphere.'

'Don't worry.' Raúl's smile brought an immediate softening to his features as he turned the full power of his charm on to the pretty blonde. 'There won't be any need for my sister-in-law to see her husband again until he's fully recovered and more able to respond to her as she deserves.'

'It would be for the best.' The sister responded to Raúl's charisma with a brilliant smile. 'Of course, if he should specifically *ask* to see her——' She paused meaningfully.

'I can be contacted on my car-phone,' he agreed in dulcet tones. 'You already have the number. Until such time as my brother is fully recovered and able to resume his role in her life, I shall be caring for Mrs Farrington.' He paused before adding in a conspiratorial undertone. 'A few newly-wed problems, you understand. Nothing serious.'

'Of course.' The sister bestowed a glowing smile on him. 'These things happen. You can depend on me to contact you at the first sign that your brother is anxious to receive visitors.'

'So you, at least, aren't incommunicado!' Nella accused furiously, after waiting for the trim figure of the sister to leave the room before venting her opinion.

'Of course not.' He looked down his long, elegant nose at her. 'I'm a businessman. The first thing I did after arriving in England was to set up lines of communication with Caracas through a London headquarters. I can't afford to live in limbo.'

'And I can, I suppose?' Nella seethed, letting her frustration have its head as he ushered her firmly from the small ward.

'It seems an ideal location to discourage you from further mischief.' He shot an angry glance at her mutinous face as she realised for the first time that the startling pale irises of his eyes were ringed with a darker colour, giving them an almost mesmeric quality against the clear white of their background.

Held entranced as he paused in his stride to glare down at her, she could only wait, breathlessly, as those eyes took their toll of her, drifting from her crown of Titian hair, past her soft hazel eyes beneath smooth, slightly arched brows, now drawn into a perplexed frown, past her small straight nose, with its delicately chiselled nostrils, to the full-lipped beauty of her small, symmetrically formed mouth above the softly rounded chin which completed the faultless oval of her face.

'I take it that in view of the reception Luis gave you, you no longer intend to continue with your feeble pretence that you've never set eyes on him before?' He showed his teeth in a smile-cum-snarl.

'And if I did?' she countered, drawing on her last reserves of courage for one desperate last-ditch battle. 'If I suggested that perhaps I bear a passing resemblance to the woman he married, that he was confused—that when he said he didn't want me it was because he realised there'd been some dreadful mistake...?' She faltered to a stop as she sensed a kind of violence stirring inside Raúl's tensely held body.

'In those circumstances I really believe I would lose my temper with you!' In the deserted corridor, he pounced on her with all the agility of a hunting jaguar, seizing her arms and turning her slender body towards him so that he could gaze directly into her troubled eyes. His soft, warm breath on her cheek frightened her as much as his softly menacing voice as his forefingers stroked her arms. 'As Luis's representative I really do believe I might be tempted to treat you like the unfaithful wife you undoubtedly are...'

'Raúl...' Her breathless exclamation combined shock and a mounting awareness of the proximity of his physical presence as she fought to control the colour which swept up beneath her pale cheeks.

'By using the palm of my hand to beat the truth out of you!' he finished grimly, the lively glitter in his narrowed eyes telling her more clearly than his words that it was an option he would take great pleasure into putting into effect if she gave him the slightest excuse.

There was a moment's silence as their eyes met and joined in battle, before he asked gently, 'Are you going to tell me that you're not the woman Luis married?'

'No.' She kept her head high as she gave him the answer he wanted. She might be in the right, but she wasn't stupid. Obviously they'd reached a stage of stalemate, where her continued denial of involvement was getting her nowhere. Far better to keep the peace, she reasoned, play her part in the scenario which had been written for her, and at the same time contact David, explain the situation and enlist his help.

'Excellent!' He approved her capitulation, a quick flare of triumph illuminating his eyes. 'Now that's settled we can return to the cottage and await Luis's full recovery.'

'Have you forgotten that he instructed you to send me away?' She jibbed fretfully as he held her hand firmly and began to make for the lift.

'He spoke from injured pride. When he recovers he'll realise that true vengeance lies in making you face up to your responsibilities.' He dismissed her quibble with a lofty wave of his free hand.

'Then, until that time, I'd prefer to stay under my brother's roof.' Her heart thumped erratically as she made the suggestion. Was her arrogant captor sufficiently persuaded of her change of heart to agree to this solution?

'*Dios*! But you try my patience when you take me for a fool!' Any faint hope she might have nurtured withered as Raúl guided her firmly into the waiting lift. 'If that's what you want, then there'd better be a bedroom there for me, because—believe me, Nella—I've no intention of letting you out of my sight until Luis is fit enough to decide what he wants to do about you.'

'You know that's impossible!' Furiously she disengaged her arm from his steel-like clamp. 'David's just starting on an election campaign which can make or break him! How could he explain your presence in his house when the local Press come nosing around? Do you want people to think you're my lover?'

For one moment she thought she'd gone too far as she raised her voice a little to make her point and thrust her chin out challengingly at him.

'Your lover, Nella?' The oiled silk of his deep voice made her flinch in embarrassment as much as the steady gaze which swept discerningly from the top of her flaming head to the tip of her fashionable cream shoes. 'Is that a proposition?'

'No, damn you! It's not!' She was shaking, more alive then than at any time during the past four years. Something that had lain dormant inside her during all that time of travail and consequent recuperation was stirring into embryonic life. Something that had no name but was akin to a life-force, moving, flexing its strength, burgeoning into a vibrant, dangerous force which, if given full rein, might even dominate her. She was scared of its latent power, bewildered by its strength. She felt like a zombie who had recovered its soul and couldn't remember how to use it. 'Whatever my sins, I've never looked twice at a married man!'

'Perhaps because once was enough to enslave the fancied ones who strayed into your path?' Raúl was regarding her strangely, with the kind of look he might have given a pet kitten had it turned round and nipped his finger, as if torn between amused surprise and the desire to chastise. 'But the situation is hypothetical, since my own life to date has been too eventful to allow me the luxury of taking a wife and raising a family.

'However, if you don't wish my presence to become an embarrassment to your brother's ambition you must accept the alternative. Tell him the truth, or at least a part of it—that you met and married Luis Farrington while you were living in Seabeach.' He shrugged broad shoulders. 'It may suit your vanity to tell him that the two of you had a lovers' quarrel and that is why you kept the news a secret, but that now Luis has been injured in an accident, you feel your place is with his family.'

'Meaning you?' she enquired drily.

The dark head nodded. 'Agree to that as a temporary measure and I'll spare you the humiliation of confessing to him about the money you appropriated.'

'And if I don't agree to go back to the cottage with you?' It was like swimming in a sea of treacle, Nella thought wildly, glad in a bizarre kind of way that her experience with Rosie had taught her how to control her mounting hysteria, and wondering detachedly what Raúl would do if she started screaming in frustration.

'You already know the answer to that.' His voice had the sharp edge of a whip as it flicked on her consciousness. 'I shall make your sins very, very public indeed.'

And pay enormous damages in libel for the privilege! Nella determined grimly. But by then the damage to David's aspirations would be irreparable.

'Well, what is it to be?' Impatiently Raúl demanded an answer as she leaned back against the corridor wall, glad that the people who passed were too intent on their own business to cast her a second glance.

There was no way Raúl could forcibly kidnap her, but if she defied him he was certainly ruthless enough to carry out his threat, she accepted miserably. Every action since his disruption of David and Charmian's dinner party proved that.

As if he'd read her thoughts, Raúl prompted her softly, 'Perhaps you don't care much what happens to your brother, whether he gets the seat in your Parliament he so desperately wants or not, but consider the alternative. In the days to come you may be very glad of his brotherly protection. It's not something you should forfeit lightly if you value your own skin and freedom, *querida.*'

'You mean, you'd respect his intervention on my behalf should he feel it necessary?' Her voice rose in astonishment as she tried to imagine herself in the part Raúl had written for her.

He nodded his dark head. 'Of course. When the time is right—when Luis has recovered enough to decide what action he wishes to take—then we shall certainly put your brother discreetly in the picture to discuss what shall be done with you in the interests of all concerned.'

'I see,' she said slowly, her brain going into top gear, her mind racing to find the least damaging solution. 'If I'm going to stay at the cottage then I'm going to need some more clothes. Do you have any objections to my telephoning David now and asking if it's convenient to go over and collect them?'

'None at all.' He regarded her speculatively. 'Do I get the feeling that you prefer to make your confession to him from a distance?'

Nella lowered her eyes, allowing her long lashes to fan her cheekbones as she murmured, 'I thought it might be preferable.' Preferable, indeed! What was preferable, she gloated delightedly, was the opportunity of speaking to David without an audience!

'*Dios*,' he muttered in heartfelt tones. 'If I were your brother I should certainly prefer to hear such news from a distance, if only to preserve me from reacting over-zealously.'

'I'm relieved you understand,' Nella said with assumed meekness. 'Naturally, when he's got over the shock, he'll want to know where I'm staying?' She lifted her voice at the end of the sentence, turning it into a question.

'Syringa Lodge, Cotteringham,' Raúl responded without hesitation.

'Right.' Nella steadied her breathing as the plan she'd made came to fruition in her mind. 'Then I'd better phone him straight away. I saw some phones downstairs on the ground floor as we came in.'

'I'm delighted you've decided to be sensible.' The dark head nodded approvingly as a gleam of triumph sparkled in the summer-sky beauty of his eyes.

'Well, I don't really have any alternative, do I?' she enquired sweetly. 'As you so rightly say, things are going to become pretty desperate for me if I alienate my own brother.'

Minutes later she was dialling David's number, praying that the gods would favour her and he would be available. She tapped her foot impatiently as she heard the number ring, conscious of Raúl prowling about in the foyer outside, and thinking how lucky she was that the old-type phone boxes had been replaced with the kind which had plastic sound-proof covers over them, so that only one person could use them at a time.

It was Charmian who answered, her voice honey-sweet as she gave the number and enquired who was calling. It was not quite so sweet when Nella identified herself and asked to speak to David.

'Is it really important? He's got his agent with him.'

'Vital!' Nella returned succinctly, amazed at the strength of her own reply, and the effect it had on her sister-in-law, who went off without further argument to fetch her husband. Whatever the result of this inexplicable interlude in her life she'd be a changed person after it, Nella decided, a strange thrill lancing through her body at the thought. She must hope that the metamorphosis and her newly found ability to handle the non-manageable would be to her advantage!

When David came to the phone she told him everything, just as it had happened.

'So you see, David,' she said as she finished, 'I don't have any option but to go along with Raúl Farrington for the time being, otherwise he's gong to create a scene which will damage both of us. And by the time it's possible to discount it, by discovering and exposing the truth of the matter, it'll be too late for you.'

'But you can't possibly go along with it! The man's mad!' David spluttered. 'Dear God, Nella—he is mad, isn't he? You didn't marry his wretched brother, did you?'

'Of course not,' she reassured him tetchily. 'And he's not mad, David, just misinformed. The marriage certificate has every appearance of being genuine, so it looks like some other woman has stolen my identity for purposes of her own—probably theft! Unfortunately, I can't actually provide an alibi for the day I was supposed to be at the register office, and Raúl is so convinced I'm lying anyway that he isn't gong to go out of his way to

give me the opportunity of trying to prove my innocence. Luis, the man who's supposed to be my husband,
has all but identified me. He's not fully conscious yet,
and heaven knows how long it will be before he recovers
fully and is able to say he made a mistake.' A dreadful
thought occurred to her. 'Of course, there's always the
possibility that he may not remember that I'm not his
wife...'

'OK.' David paused, obviously deep in thought. 'You
say you feel it's quite safe to go back to this—this Syringa
Lodge with Raúl Farrington?'

'Absolutely,' Nella assured him firmly. 'His credentials are impeccable.' Laughter gurgled in her throat as
she added inconsequentially and a trifle hysterically, 'His
ancestors fought with Bolivar!'

'Right. Leave it to me, then, Nella. The next twenty-
one days before the voting at the by-election are absolutely critical to me, and we don't want the least bit of
scandal or gossip to be circulated about the family, so
there's not much I can do personally. But I'll speak to
my solicitor in strict confidence and get him to engage
a private detective in an effort to trace the girl who mas-
queraded as you. Unless it's a deliberate dirty-tricks
campaign waged by some of my opponents—which is
most unlikely—I imagine Seabeach is the best place to
start, but I'll leave that to the experts.'

'I hadn't thought of that, David.' Nella bit her lip.
'You mean I might have been set up solely to discredit
you?'

'It's possible, but unlikely,' he agreed. 'If that was the
case I imagine the newspapers would have received copies
of the marriage certificate by now. No, almost certainly
it's based on fraud. Hopefully the whole thing can be
sorted out within a few days. If not, once the by-

election's over I'll come over to the cottage and challenge Farrington face-to-face. Win or lose, mud won't hurt me then—particularly as it isn't going to stick in the long run!'

'That's wonderful, David!' Relief flooded through Nella's system and echoed in her voice. 'I knew you'd come up with something. In the meantime I'll get Raúl to drive me over to pick up a change of clothes. I'll let him believe that I've told you I truly am his sister-in-law, but I'm keeping a low profile so as not to detract from your campaign.'

'Bless you.' The relief in his voice was evident. 'Charmian and I mightn't be here when you arrive. We're leaving in a few minutes to do a tour of the constituency—to get our campaign underway. You know the kind of thing—shaking hands with local party workers and kissing babies...' He paused, then said uncertainly, 'Look, Nella, I appreciate what you're doing for me, but I can only agree if I'm certain you're in no danger. Are you sure you'll be all right alone in that cottage with Farrington? Because if you've got any doubts——'

'None at all, David,' she returned firmly. 'His only concern is to keep me safe and secure until such time as his brother is fit enough to discuss our future, and I'm banking on the hope that long before then the real culprit will have been identified!'

'Right. And speaking of banking, I'll notify *your* bank to be on the alert for anyone trying to make withdrawals from your account or issuing cheques on it, and you'll promise to get in touch with me or my agent at the first sign of Farrington treating you with anything but total respect?'

'I promise.' She gave him the assurance he needed, crossing her fingers childishly, so that the oath wasn't binding. Whatever happened, she could hang in there for three weeks!

After wishing him good luck at the hustings, and assuring him she had a key to his front door, she replaced the receiver decisively on its rest. Well, she thought, squaring her shoulders belligerently as she stepped outside the booth, the die was cast. For better or worse, she had handed over the next few days of her life into Raúl Farrington's keeping.

'Well?' Immediately he was at her side.

'No problems.' She smiled faintly. 'Naturally he was surprised, not to say flabbergasted at the news, and not particularly happy that I hadn't confided in him earlier. But he's accepted the situation and is obviously relieved that I've no intentions of making a public announcement about my new status.'

'And there'll be no problem about collecting your clothes?'

'None. Although the house will probably be empty when we arrive, so you won't have the opportunity of exchanging familial greetings,' she added drily.

'In the circumstances, just as well.' Raúl shot her a scathing glance. 'Let's get moving, then!'

The beautiful detached house showed no signs of occupancy as the Jaguar came to a halt in the driveway.

'Will you wait in the car or do you want to come inside with me?' Nella offered the options, her voice devoid of expression.

'I'll wait here.' He tossed her a smile which she found oddly disturbing. 'It's not so much that I trust you, Nella, but it's obvious you are a woman who knows which side of her bread is buttered. I have no fears that you'll abscond.'

'I compliment you on your knowledge of idiomatic English,' she told him with a sarcastic lift of her eyebrows. 'Your command of the language is excellent.'

He bowed his dark head, accepting the compliment as his due. 'It's a tradition in our family to speak fluent English in honour of the first John Farrington, who fought beside the Liberator. My children, too, will be fluent in the tongue of their noble ancestor.'

'You put such value on mercenaries in Venezuela?' Nella found herself unable to resist the taunt as she spared a fleeting thought for Raúl's offspring. Sons, undoubtedly, she decided, acknowledging his flagrant prejudice without remorse. Daughters would hold a lesser tenure in the affections of her opinionated captor.

'Not mercenaries!' His light eyes flashed with the stripping power of a laser beam. 'Heroes of the Liberation! In Caracas they are still honoured, the British battalions who fought so bravely beside Simón Bolivar to overthrow the oppressors, their names engraved on monuments erected in their honour.' His piercing gaze, haughty and remote, pinned her face. 'It may be completely unknown in your country, but the British enjoy a singular honour in Venezuela. Their army is permitted to enter the country with fixed bayonets. The only case I know in modern history where a foreign power may enter another armed.'

'An honour, indeed,' she accorded placatingly, keeping to herself the opinion that it was one which was unlikely to be utilised in modern times, unless of course, it referred to ceremonial guards. 'I'll try not to keep you waiting too long.'

As she'd suspected, David and Charmian had already left. Speeding upstairs to the bedroom she'd been allocated, she offered up a brief prayer for David's success.

Despite their lack of true closeness, she knew him to be a good and honest man. One who would serve his constituents well.

A rueful smile turned the corners of her mouth as her mind flitted back to the past. How ironical that, having eventually regained some emotional equilibrium after the shadowy, illogical world she'd inhabited with Rosie, she'd been plunged into this bizarre situation!

Dragging out her suitcase from the bottom of the wardrobe, she began to pack methodically. Underclothes, a nightdress—pretty, but far less glamorous than the one Raúl had provided—three summer dresses, a couple of skirts, a pair of pale stone-washed jeans, and a T-shirt. In line with her previous lifestyle they were of good quality, but purchased locally and at reasonable prices. A dark quilted jacket in case the weather changed, flat canvas casuals, a pair of beige sandals and a frivolous pair of high-heeled white sandals which she'd bought in a sale, on impulse, and never worn. A selection of her normal make-up and her toiletries gathered from the bathroom and crammed in a sponge-bag completed her packing.

Finally, before leaving, she left a brief note for her erstwhile hosts, confirming that she'd collected her belongings. On the threshold she hesitated, experiencing a cool shiver of apprehension trembling down her spine, a premonition that she was leaving David and Charmian's house for the last time as a member of the Lambert family.

Valiantly she made the effort to expunge the sensation from her mind. Three weeks, she reminded herself sturdily. Three weeks at the very most, and her ordeal would be ended.

# CHAPTER SIX

'THAT didn't take you long.' Raúl was standing by the Jaguar waiting for her, and took her case and put it into the boot.

'I didn't need much time.' Nella slid into the front passenger seat and fastened her seatbelt. 'I don't envisage that you're going to introduce me to a hectic social life.'

'Why not?' His laconic reply amazed her. 'I wouldn't want you to become bored with my company.'

'I don't think that's possible,' she returned fervently, immediately regretting her outburst as he shot her a quickly assessing glance before easing his long length into the driver's seat.

'I'm flattered.' He accepted her comment as a compliment, as she'd feared he would. 'Since we now understand each other, shall we declare a cessation of hostilities until Luis is fully recovered, and make the most of what I understand to be unusually pleasant weather in this country?'

'Fine by me.' Turning her gaze, she regarded his averted profile with a mixture of relief and resignation, only too pleased to discuss other things in place of her supposed relationship with Luis. 'But you do our weather an injustice. It's a great deal pleasanter than most people give us credit for—possibly because we always seem to be complaining about it, I suppose,' she added, in fairness to his assumption.

'But then I'm a harsh judge,' he responded lightly. 'Venezuela is known as the Land of Eternal Spring.'

'An evocative title,' Nella agreed, quite happy to discuss the non-contentious subject of meteorology. 'And one I suppose Luis was able to capitalise on in his job?'

'Undoubtedly a good marketing point.' He nodded agreeably. 'How familiar are you with this part of the country?'

Nella cast him a quick glance of apprehension, suspicious of his motive in asking the question.

'Not very,' she admitted, keeping her voice level with an effort. 'David and Charmian moved down here about six years ago, but until my grandmother died I lived with her in a small village called Lowdale Heath in Cambridgeshire.' His set profile told her nothing as she added, 'In the south-east of England.'

'Go on,' he invited her, the timbre of his voice flat, telling her nothing of his feelings. 'I'm interested to know your background. Tell me more. Do you have other brothers and sisters?'

'No, just David.' She smiled wryly, acknowledging her own sense of isolation. 'We've never been all that close because our father walked out on our mother when David was fourteen and I was just four. Two years later he asked her for a divorce and we never saw him again. Rosie, my mother's mother that was, looked after me so that Mother could go out to work, and David was sent away to boarding school. When I was eighteen Mother remarried and emigrated to Australia with her new husband, and I went to college to study modern languages.'

'You intended becoming a teacher, perhaps?' Raúl made no effort to hide the surprise in his voice. Was it because he suspected she was lying about her accomplishments?

'Actually, I wanted to work as an interpreter,' she told him evenly. 'But two years after Mother emigrated Rosie showed the first signs of Alzheimer's disease. I couldn't possibly have left her, so I decided to try to find a job I could do from home. Luckily someone at the college introduced me to a publisher who was looking for a competent translator. The money wasn't marvellous, but at least it enabled me to stay where I was needed.'

'Highly commendable,' Raúl said with a silky smoothness which betokened that he hadn't believed one word of her explanation. 'Then what happened?'

'My grandmother lived for two years after the onset of the illness.' Nella bit her lip in an effort to restrain her tears. Such a simple sentence, yet it concealed so much heartbreak and pain. No one, not having lived with a sufferer from such a mind-destroying affliction, could possibly understand the drastic effect it could have on the sanity of a carer who accepted twenty-four-hours-a-day responsibility—especially when that loved one occupied such a permanent and treasured place in that carer's heart!

'She died two years ago, then, is that right?'

'Full marks for arithmetic!' She felt sorry for her rudeness the moment the words had left her lips, but it was too late to retract them so she went on doggedly, 'After the funeral a friend of mine invited me to spend a week with her and her children at Seabeach Holiday Camp. I thought it would give me a chance to consider my future.'

'And you found it working as a menial at the camp, hmm?'

'If that's what you want to call it.' Nella shrugged off
his sarcasm. Being in charge of the children's play ac-
tivities had been physically and mentally demanding, but
refreshing after the upside-down illogicality of the half-
life she'd shared with Rosie. 'I enjoyed the work and,
of course, I was still doing the translating job, which
meant I was able to stay at Seabeach in the winter months
when the camp was closed. Cheap off-season accommodation was reasonably easy to find.'

'And a rich husband even easier. *Dios*!' he swore sav-
agely under his breath. 'Luis with his Latin charm, his
adolescent innocence and profligate spending habits must
have seemed like God's gift to you.' He cast her a bitter
look, his eyes narrowed like a tiger sizing up its prey.
'One look from your artless butterscotch eyes, one word
from your voluptuous lips and my spoiled younger
brother would have been as malleable in your delicate
hands as a lump of plasticine left in the sun.'

'Do I detect jealousy?' A warm wave of colour washed
over Nella's face as she was stung to an acid retort.

A harsh bark of laughter met her accusation. 'I have
no need to be jealous of a boy! Had I been with him
that night in the pub where you met he would never have
got to first base with you. Believe me, *querida*, I would
have given you everything he gave you—and more. But
never my bank account or my name!'

If he hadn't been driving she would have smacked his
arrogant face in answer to his derogatory comments. As
it was, Nella fought to control the kind of rage she'd
never felt before. Placid, they'd called her at school;
amenable had been her tag at Seabeach, but now those
qualities, if they'd ever existed, were splintering into
shards to give way to an emotion much more violent and
dangerous. For a moment she became the girl he sup-

posed her to be, laughing and enjoying herself in some
public house, imagining herself to be confronted by the
pleasant-looking young man she'd first seen stretched
out on a hospital bed, and beside him the tough-boned,
hard-muscled intolerant individual who was driving the
Jaguar with all the fiery intensity of a war-lord bent on
destruction.

'And what makes you think for one moment,' she
asked in a cool, dispassionate voice which camouflaged
her icy anger, 'that I would have looked in your direction for even the space of one nano-second?'

'Because I know your kind of woman,' he answered
her rawly. 'I know what switches you on and what
switches you off. I've seen your eyes glow at the promise
of some golden bauble, your pretty lips purse seductively at the sight of a bulging wallet. I've heard your
whimpered promises and love-sick sighs and felt your
tender little hands trying to reach my heart through the
sensitivity of my skin...' Savagery edged each word,
sharpening them so that they fell painfully on Nella's
ears. 'None of you has succeeded, but believe me, I know
your game and I can play it as artfully, but more skil-
fully. If I had wanted you, Nella, I would have taken
you. Believe it.'

She almost did. Only some deep awareness she couldn't
even understand prompted her to amend his audacious
claim. He wouldn't have taken her, or any other woman
for that matter, unless she had pronounced herself
willing. If she hadn't believed that she would have been
terrified. For one brief, fractured slice of time she actually imagined herself disrobed and willing beneath
Raúl's naked body, felt in her imagination his hot, sweet
breath on her face, his steady, purposeful hands
worshipping her breasts, his predatory mouth claiming

and possessing her soft, yielding mouth... And felt a wash of colour rise from her breasts to her hairline.

Horrified by the temporary feelings which had invaded her, she eased her seatbelt so that she could turn sideways, the easier to fasten her gaze on the stony contours of his bold nose and achingly beautiful mouth. From this angle the cleft in his chin looked as if it had been gouged out by a too-avidly wielded chisel. Only the long dark lashes which hid his eyes from her lent any softness to a face which denied that its possessor knew the meaning of charity.

'You vaunt your ignorance of women when you speak so scornfully of us,' she addressed his hawklike profile hotly. 'You speak of a world of violence, domination and fear. Luis, for all his naïveté, is loving and trusting and decent. No woman worthy of the name would choose you in preference to him!'

'Not even you?' Quick as a dart from a champion's hand, the words struck her.

Her riposte ricocheted back before she had time to consider how he would translate it. 'Particularly me!' she vowed.

'Excellent, *querida*,' he said smoothly, with no trace of anger in his silky voice. 'It seems you may have some feeling for your husband after all.' He turned a corner and braked. 'We're arrived.'

Nella swung round to find to her astonishment that they were parked near a cliff-top, with a marvellous view of the sea, shining opalescent beneath the hot kiss of the early afternoon sun.

'We're at the coast...' she said stupidly, wondering how she'd managed to stay unaware of their progress, shocked that her mind had been so easily distracted. Wearily she pushed one hand through her hair, feeling her forehead damp where the russet tendrils lay in mild disorder. Thank heavens she'd taken the opportunity to change into something fresh at David's house, she thought with relief. Prepared for the heat, she'd dressed simply in a blue and white spotted cotton dress, short sleeved, V-necked, the skirt shaped to her waist and lightly gored for freedom of movement.

'I love the sea.' Raúl was staring out of the wind-screen, eyes narrowed against the glare, his tone softly conversational now. 'I find it has a tranquillising effect in a world of disruption.'

'Me too.' Gratefully Nella followed his lead, feeling as if she were walking on hot coals, afraid of treading too firmly for fear of being hurt. 'Where you live, in Caracas, is that near the sea?' she ventured quietly, hoping to extend the mood of calmness which appeared to have descended on him.

'Caracas is inland.' He was still staring thoughtfully at the expanse of water below them. 'The port is at La Guaira. You have to drive through the mountains to reach it, but it's an industrial town, not noted for its beauty. I have a place outside of Caracas, in the hills, where it is very beautiful, and a holiday home on the island of Margarita.' He cast her a sidelong glance. 'But I suppose Luis has already told you about that?'

'No.' Nella denied it simply.

'You surprise me.' To her astonishment he accepted her word. 'It's one of his favourite hang-outs. "Margarita—the pearl of the Caribbean",' he quoted, as if from a brochure, a slight edge sharpening his tone. 'It was one of the resorts he was over here to promote, although, to be honest, there are other parts of Venezuela which would benefit more from increased tourism. Margarita has much in common with a beautiful woman—give her too much attention and you will ruin her.'

Nella sighed. Just her luck to find herself the prisoner of the king of male chauvinists. 'You obviously have a lot of experience in such matters,' she commented wryly, as he opened the door and strode round to her side of the car.

'Being rejected at the age of nineteen by a girl who swore she loved me more than life itself, in favour of a fat pig of a man whose sole attraction was the size of his bank balance, was the only experience I needed.' He held out a peremptory hand to assist her.

'Thank you.' Accepting the courtesy with a slight nod of her head, Nella suppressed a smile at the extent of his arrogance. 'It didn't occur to you that your rival might possess other qualities you lacked?' she enquired innocently, an inner sense of mischief tempting her to tease him. 'Like charm? Humility? Experience?'

'No.' His light eyes sparkled as he dismissed the suggestion out of hand. 'He was superior to me in one way only—the size of the fortune he had accumulated.'

'How humiliating for you.' Nella conjured up a sympathetic smile, beginning to enjoy herself as his eyebrows drew together. 'Perhaps being a bad judge of women runs in your family?'

'Every man is entitled to one mistake, *querida*.' The insolence of his tone was reflected in the coldness of his expression. 'Fortunately, unlike my brother, I hadn't been stupid enough to enter into a commitment when I made mine.' He passed discerning eyes over her uncovered skin before saying abruptly, 'We have a walk ahead of us before we reach the place I have in mind for lunch. Will you burn?'

Taken aback by the unexpected question she grimaced down at her unfashionably pale arms. 'There's some protective cream in my case,' she informed him, adding stiffly, 'Thank you for reminding me. Where exactly are we going?'

'An open-air restaurant I discovered the afternoon I was driving around looking for a suitable house to rent. It's in a small lane which leads through a wood to a wild and isolated boulder beach.' His smile wasn't pleasant. 'The fresh air and exercise will do you good.'

The implication was that both were alien to her way of life. She quashed the impulse to contradict him, merely adding yet another black mark to the record of the girl who had dared to borrow her identity.

'Walking's fine by me.' She shrugged her shoulders, glad that she was wearing flat-heeled sandals as she added ironically, 'How sweet of you to show such concern for my well-being.'

'*De nada*.' He waved her sarcastic gratitude aside. 'In my brother's absence, your protection is my concern. You may well be about to suffer for your sins, but I have no intention of seeing you become a burnt offering.' He unlocked and opened the boot, indicating the interior. 'Do whatever's necessary to retain your dewy freshness.'

Nella obeyed him, applying the cool lotion to every part of her exposed skin: face, neck, arms and finally her legs, reaching to her ankles to smooth it upward to her knees, conscious that every movement she made was being observed by the steadfast gaze of her companion. Dabbing two final portions on her insteps, which she knew from past experience could become painfully burned, she straightened up, sweeping her own eyes over Raúl's golden skin.

Despite the fairness of his eyes, his complexion spoke of his Latin American heritage. The Land of Eternal Spring... An evocative description which suggested temperatures at least as high as those of Devon on a summer day. Still, it was better to be safe.

'Do you need any?' She offered the bottle to him.

'Do I?' He returned the question, inviting her inspection. 'What do you think?'

An odd pang of uneasiness afflicted her as she realised intuitively that if she said yes he was going to invite her to apply it for him. Of course she would refuse, she determined stoutly, the tips of her fingers already itching in anticipation of the forbidden pleasure of touching his skin, and of course he would guess at the reason for her refusal.

She shook her head. 'You look tough enough to cope without it,' she told him carelessly, hiding her expression from him as she turned to replace the container in the car.

'Oh, I am, Nella.' His voice was softly menacing. 'You won't ever want to meet anyone tougher. Shall we go?'

They walked in silence, the downhill journey easy as the slight breeze stirred against their skins and played with the soft tendrils of Nella's hair.

The first sign that there was a restaurant hidden in the narrow lane, with its shady banks of rhododendrons and softly rustling trees, came when, on turning a particularly sharp bend, she saw a small, arrowed notice advertising cream teas pointing to a narrow gap in the hedge.

'Oh, this is lovely!' Accepting Raúl's invitation to precede him through a wicket gate, she made no secret of her delight as they entered a large garden, beautifully landscaped with shrubs and weeping willow trees. A dozen or so tables already laid for lunch were arranged on a centre lawn in front of an old thatched bungalow, its walls a mass of purple wistaria.

'So I thought.' Raúl ushered her towards a table. 'A place for connoisseurs, no? Away from the summer crowds? From what Luis told me about you I supposed you preferred the bright lights and loud music.'

'Not I.' Nella denied the assumption without bothering to expand upon it. 'I much prefer solitude. It's always seemed strange to me that so many people prefer to sit together rather than to walk a few metres to find their own space. The more accessible beaches along the coast by Torquay will be packed on a day like this—and the restaurants too.'

'Whereas here, for the price of a stroll, one can lunch in peace.' He offered her a menu. 'I hope the food won't be too simple for your exotic taste.'

'What, no escargots?' Irritated by his condescending tone, she aped a moue of disappointment, as a wild temptation flared in her imagination. Some wretched girl had dared to take on her identity and dump her in this mess, so why didn't she act out the part she'd been landed with? It would only be for a short period of time, until David's detective discovered the truth, and it'd be a good deal less frustration than wincing every time Raúl made her the butt of his scorn!

'And the smoked salmon's off!' She fluttered her eyelashes across the table at him. 'Oh dear, in that case I'd better have the prawn salad with new potatoes, served with freshly baked rolls and Devon butter, washed down by cider and followed by strawberries and thick Devon cream!' She handed the menu back to him with a serene smile. 'And coffee,' she added as an afterthought. 'Freshly ground, of course.'

'Of course.'

Had she detected a flare of amusement in his eyes before he'd walked away to place the order? Nella leaned back in her chair, luxuriating in the warmth of the sun. Had Rosie's doctor been right in his diagnosis that her personality had been repressed, her spirit dampened by the responsibility of looking after Rosie? she mused. Dear Michael, who'd reluctantly supported her wish not to have her grandmother confined to the local geriatric hospital, expressing his admiration for her determination to do her best for the elderly woman...

Later, when he'd discovered her weeping after Rosie's funeral, he'd held her in his arms and comforted her as if she'd been a child, stroking her arms and kissing the top of her head, advising her to take a long, relaxing break, to learn to deal with life as it really was, not as it had appeared in the disordered mind of a sick woman. And she'd obeyed him, but somehow her spirit had remained stunted... until now. Until she'd found herself plunged into another nightmare. Only this time it was different. This time her antagonist was a man in the prime of his life, mentally and physically sound, and this time she was not going to allow herself to be crushed.

It was two hours later when she drained the final drops of coffee from her cup, and Raúl called for and settled the bill before rising from his seat to place his hand firmly beneath her elbow. 'Time to go, Nella,' he exhorted firmly.

'Must we?' Getting into the role of the character she'd decided to play, she painted a pout on her curvaceous mouth. 'Why can't we just sit here?'

'Because by the time you come face-to-face with Luis again I mean to have brought a little discipline into your disordered life!' he commanded impatiently.

'Brute!' Her eyes flashed her contempt at him before she realised that his opinion of Luis's real wife was well-merited. 'Besides,' she added, suddenly inspired, 'you heard what Luis said in the hospital. He told you he didn't want me. He asked you to send me away.'

'Hardly surprising, was it?' he enquired acidly. 'I wasn't anticipating a joyous reunion. My only reason for taking you there was to let him know that I'd caught up with you. To give him the peace of mind of knowing that you'd be required to make recompense for your sins! He'll be happy enough to see you again when he realises he'll have you at his mercy. Now, *vamos*!'

She went, concealing her small smile of satisfaction at the way she had managed to rile him.

Although Raúl had described what lay ahead, he'd been unable to do verbal justice to the scene which, forty minutes later, unfolded before her as they walked along a path which twisted and turned through woodlands beneath a canopy of leaves which filtered the strong sunlight into brilliant, piercing rays. After the heat of the dusty road it was a cool haven of silence, broken only by the sound of the nearby sea.

As the trees thinned and the ground dipped sharply Nella saw the beach, and gasped. Raúl had called it a boulder beach, but even so she hadn't been prepared for the size of the boulders, some of them over a metre in height. Small, indeed—just an inlet between two arms of the surrounding cliff—it was in total shade. Not a rendezvous for children or sunbathers, she accorded, acknowledging the reason for its isolation, but breathtakingly, threateningly beautiful.

Thrusting her feet out of her sandals, the urge to paddle an irresistible compulsion, she moved forward, only to find her passage barred by Raúl.

'Be careful. It's dangerous.' His restraining hand on her arm held her immobile.

'I just want to cool my feet,' she protested, raising her eyes pleadingly to his adamant face as the breeze caught and lifted her hair, sending it bouncing against her shoulders.

'Then we'll go together.'

He scrambled with her down the rocky outcrop, holding her arm firmly as she sprang across the boulders, their cold smoothness a welcome balm to her hot skin. His own canvas shoes were soaking as the waves creamed their way into the shore, before streaming back in hissing runlets to their source.

Her problems momentarily forgotten as the waves slapped their cold caress against her ankles, Nella cried out with pleasure, lifting her face to the sky, abandoning herself to the pulse of nature which thrummed in the turmoil around her.

'Have you had enough?' Several minutes later the soft question brought her back to her senses, forcing her to awareness of the man standing beside her, his steadying grasp like a band of iron round her arm, reminding her that he wasn't as suitably garbed for water sports as she.

'I'm sorry.' She glanced down at his wet shoes, at the expanse of bare skin above them where he'd turned up the bottoms of his trousers, the edge of the latter now dark with salt-water. 'Your clothes are wet.'

'They'll dry.' He dismissed her apology with a shrug. 'Be careful how you walk. If you fell and broke your ankle I would have a long walk back with you in my arms.'

'A fate to be avoided by all means,' she agreed lightly, reading a double meaning into the tersely spoken sentence. 'Don't worry. I'm pretty agile.'

She proved it by gaining the shore without trouble, clambering up the rough scree and regaining possession of her sandals without incident.

'Where to now?' she asked, straightening her back after adjusting the heel straps, and turning to face him.

'That rather depends on you, Nella.' He was staring at her, a strange expression on his face as his eyes met and held hers. 'What do you want to do?'

'I hadn't thought...' Her voice tailed away as every cell in her body seemed to become charged with an inner electricity. Was this what a Christmas tree felt like when lit up for the festival? she thought hysterically. Special and glowing? She licked lips which were parched, tasting the salt before wiping her hand across her forehead, feeling its heated dampness.

'Perhaps you should.' The short stride he took brought him within a few centimetres of where she stood, so that she could feel the animal heat of his body bouncing off her own skin.

Bewildered by the cloying aura which seemed to have imprisoned her in its thrall, she thrust her hands into her hair, shaking her head as if to release herself from the strange spell which beset her, but the atmosphere seemed to grow more tense, the surrounding trees and shrubs more expectant. Disturbed, she raised one hand to touch the opposite arm, where Raúl's fingers had left an invisible imprint.

He followed the movement with dreamy eyes before raising his hand and displacing her fingers with his own. Ignoring her small, quiet mew of protest, he placed his other hand behind her neck, drawing her into his body, his fingers threading through the soft Titian veil of her hair, supporting her head as he lowered his mouth and took her lips with a feverish intensity.

She couldn't—mustn't respond! But the reflex action of her body was overpowering her mind as Raúl's tongue flirted with her own. She was melting, dissolving like an ice cube in a summer drink, incapable of rational thought. One step back and her pliant body was held against the rigid trunk of a tree, her legs spread, her feet eased between the tangled roots. There was nowhere for her to go. No way of escaping the gently persuasive seduction of Raúl's powerful body as he eased it against her, his thighs hard against hers, his chest moving gently but persuasively against her breasts, taunting them into erectile resistance.

She tried to protest, but he swallowed her complaint, moving his head sideways, deepening the kiss, so that her hands had to leave their defensive position on his shoulders and drop behind his back. She was burning with an inner fire, fed by the body heat of the virile male whose every touch was torment. Her own body was screaming for permission to surrender. Only one cool, isolated part of her brain shouted danger, preached caution.

It was the sudden hard surge of Raúl's maleness against her yielding flesh that broke the spell and spurred her into action.

She began to fight him, twisting and turning, her body sliding down the trunk. Her breathing laboured, somehow she managed to drag her mouth away from his predatory possession, to cry out her rejection in the one way she could be sure he would accept it.

'Stop it! Stop it!' she sobbed. 'I'm your brother's wife! I'm Luis's wife!'

Every taut line of Raúl's face and body proclaimed his arousal, yet his eyes were diamond-hard, brilliant as midsummer stars in a cloudless sky, as he stood away,

giving her the space she demanded, dragging his regard
from the top of her tousled head to her pale, sea-washed
toes, and back again to centre its contempt on her desperate face.

'At last,' he said with consummate satisfaction. 'At
last, I've found the way to make you say it out loud.'

# CHAPTER SEVEN

IT HAD been a fiendishly cruel move on Raúl's part and she hated him for it. No, that wasn't true. Resented was a better word for the way she felt about him. Moodily Nella lifted her left foot from the surrounding bath-water and regarded the blister on her big toe where the strap of her sandal had rubbed the skin away. If she'd needed to be punished for her mindless surrender to Raúl's ruthless seduction technique, then what better retribution than having to walk two kilometres with the salty residue of the English Channel stinging the wound in her foot every step of the way!

Even then the pain had been secondary to that in her heart, and that was the most frightening thing of all. With the speed of drops of cold water falling on a baking-tray straight out of the oven, her mind skittered away from dignifying her feelings for the arrogant Venezuelan with the word 'love'. Yet caught in his arms, her heart pounding against the formidable strength of his body, she had almost persuaded herself that the powerful emotions controlling her reactions had their origin in something deeper than mere physical attraction.

How was it possible to respond emotionally to someone who treated you with such contempt, when all she'd felt for kind, caring, considerate Michael, who had always been on call when Rosie had needed sedation, had been a comfortable friendship? Yet she'd loved her grandmother despite the bitter, cruel accusations Rosie's disturbed mind had forced to her lips, particularly towards the end of her illness. Oh, she'd wept out her pain in the small dark hours of the morning often enough, because her emotional skin had never grown tough enough to shrug off the insults, but she'd understood the cause behind the abuse and had never let the hurt she felt damage her enduring love for her grandmother, because it had been based on a misunderstanding.

In the same way she could understand Raúl's attitude towards her. He was entitled to feel bitterness towards the woman whom he had every reason to believe had treated his younger brother so appallingly.

Despite the warmth of the water, she shivered as she recalled the earlier silent march back to the car. Raúl had made no concessions to her shorter stride or the uphill gradient on the return journey, and she'd had to grit her teeth against the pain of the blister as she'd loped along in a half-run in an effort to keep up with him, too proud to draw attention to her infirmity or to ask him to moderate his pace because of it.

At least, she opined philosophically, her lie had earned her a pass of safe conduct, and for that she should be grateful. Now all she had to do was go along with her false confession until such time as the truth emerged. Yet she'd already stopped protesting her innocence, so why had Raúl gone to such extremes to force her confession? Thoughtfully she gathered a handful of the perfumed rainbow-hued bubbles surrounding her and let them dribble down over her breasts, inhaling their subtle perfume as they burst against her soft nipples.

David would hire the best help available on her behalf, and her non-involvement should be relatively simple to prove. Signatures, for instance; the other woman must have signed the withdrawal form at the bank and the certificate at the register office. Even if the interloper had managed to get a copy of her own signature, an expert wouldn't be fooled by a forgery, she comforted herself. Of course, the best evidence of all would be a photograph, but logic told her that that would be an unlikely bonus. The ceremony had been a rushed one, with no guests and strangers as witnesses, Luis having been eager to thwart any interference from Raúl, and the girl he'd married anxious to conceal her true identity. No, even if Luis had insisted on taking his own photographs as a memento, the false Nella would have ensured the film was never printed! Besides, if Luis had had any prints, either in the car or at his apartment, Raúl would have discovered them and she wouldn't be here now.

No, she would have to put her faith in David's solicitor and hope that the next time she was allowed to see Luis the latter would realise she was a stranger.

Gracefully she rose to her feet, reaching for the soft blue bath-towel, wrapping it round herself as she stepped from the bath. A week at the most, she hazarded optimistically, and she could be back in David and Charmian's pleasant house and miles away from the dark threat posed by her South American captor. For so brief a time surely she could act out the lie she'd told? Heaven knew she'd acted out enough of Rosie's troubled fantasies in the past in an effort to keep her dearly loved grandmother if not happy, then momentarily free from distress.

Carefully she patted her injured toe dry, before covering it with a clean tissue as reluctantly she acknowledged a feeling of respect for the way Raúl had reacted to his brother's predicament. A lesser man could easily have let him face the consequences of his stupidity alone. Despite Raúl's tough attitude, he clearly cared deeply for his brother's welfare and was far more tender-hearted than he was prepared to admit—at least, she qualified, to her.

Gaining her bedroom, she flopped down on the bed. The sea-air and the warm bath had made her feel sleepy. She glanced at the door. Not surprisingly there was no keyhole in it and therefore no key. Still, confident that her position as Raúl's *cuñada* provided all the protection she needed from his potent sexuality, she covered her warm body with her own broderie anglais nightdress before stretching out on top of the duvet, her hair spread on the pillow in an effort to keep her face and neck cool.

She awakened to the sound of a sharp knocking on her door and struggled to sit up. Seven o'clock in the evening, according to her watch, which she'd abandoned on the bedside table! And the master was demanding to be fed!

'Wait a moment!' Quickly she curled her body up and slid it beneath the duvet to preserve her modesty, although in all honesty her nightdress had all the simplicity and innocence of a child's summer dress.

'May I enter?'

He was going to whether she gave permission or not. She could hear the intent in his voice.

'If you must.' Better with permission than without.

'I've brought you a cup of tea.' The fact was self-evident, but totally surprising as for the first time Nella realised that her throat was parched.

'I thought South Americans drank coffee,' she said in surprise as Raúl placed a small tray containing a cup of rich golden-brown tea, a separate milk jug, a sugar bowl and a saucer containing several slices of lemon on the bedside table.

'We do,' he affirmed equably. 'But that doesn't preclude us from enjoying other beverages. Tea-drinking is
a time-honoured custom in my own family. We drink it
with lemon, but I understand the British prefer milk.'

Nella shrugged. 'I'm easy,' she said, then immediately
regretted her words, unable to prevent an embarrassed
blush pinkening her cheeks as, recognising the possible
*double entendre*, she amended swiftly, 'I mean, I prefer
milk in winter, but in summer I find lemon more
refreshing.'

Quickly she reached for the tray, seizing a slice of
lemon and squeezing it into the contents of the cup.

'Good. I'm glad I was able to anticipate your pleasure.'

To her consternation Raúl sat down on the bed as she
lifted the cup to her lips. Unable to keep her hold on
the duvet, it slid down to her waist as she sipped the
fragrant liquid. Not until she'd tasted it did she realise
just how much she had needed its refreshing stimu-
lation. She kept her eyes downcast, aware via a sixth
sense that she was the object of Raúl's steady appraisal,
and uneasy beneath his unwavering contemplation.

Was she being psychotic of had she detected an under-
current of a different meaning in his remark about anticipating her pleasure? Her flush deepened as she
resolutely sipped the scalding-hot tea. Please God, her
companion would put down her rise in temperature to
the effect of the steam which was dampening her face
rather than to its true cause—the remembrance of that
disturbing interlude in the woods.

Her hand began to shake, so she had no option but
to replace the cup on the tray. 'I'm sorry,' she gasped.
'But I'll have to let it cool down a little before
finishing it.'

'There's no hurry.' There was mocking laughter in his eyes as he observed her flushed face closely. 'Our table is reserved for nine.'

'We're eating out? Did you find my cooking so unpalatable?' She made no attempt to hide her surprise. The last thing she'd expected was that her immediate future would include a social outing.

'Let's just say that I feel the need to relax a little among congenial company, and I'm fortunate enough to have been given an introduction to a private members' club not too far from here.'

'That sounds a bit dull to me.' Piqued by the gibe about seeking congenial company, Nella made a gesture of distaste before adding for good measure, 'Still, I forget you're so much older than Luis.'

'And wiser, more experienced and sophisticated.' His smile wasn't particularly pleasant, and it gave her an odd thrill knowing she'd touched him on the raw. 'So if your idea of amusement is belting out songs from the shows in concert with a karaoke machine——' he began disdainfully.

'It isn't,' Nella interrupted him, victim of a surge of honesty, her eyes bright with inward laughter. 'Unfortunately when singing voices were distributed I was at the end of the queue. I was the only girl in the class at my school who was instructed under pain of punishment to mouth the words of the school song instead of attempting to sing them.' She sighed reminiscently. 'You can't get much worse than that.'

'And I suppose you've got two left feet as well, when it comes to dancing?' Dark eyebrows slanted enquiringly.

She shrugged. 'Let's just say I'm a bit out of practice.'

'But no doubt it will come back to you as soon as you feel the rhythm throbbing through your blood?'

'Probably,' she returned shortly, irritated by his caustic tone. Dancing had always come naturally to her. At college she'd been a regular attendant at the student discos and the small, intimate clubs with their live groups, finding a marvellous release from the tension of studying in the vigorous freedom of movement. During the past four years there'd been little opportunity to indulge herself but, like riding a bicycle, dancing was an enduring skill. 'Does it matter?'

'It could, if I felt the urge to take the floor myself.'

Nella frowned. 'You mean, we're going to some kind of night club?'

'Isn't that what I just said?'

It hadn't been. But before she could point out that she'd assumed that a private club meant merely a private *dining* club, he moved abruptly, rising from the bed with such momentum that he dragged the duvet a few centimetres with him.

Before she could prevent it a sharp cry of pain left Nella's lips as the material moved roughly across her sore toe.

'What is it?' Raúl spun round to regard her, frowning as he saw her wince with pain. 'Are you unwell?'

'No,' she reassured him, hastily then, observing his frown deepen as if in disbelief, found herself confessing with a degree of embarrassment, 'It's nothing really, just that this afternoon's walk left me with the legacy of a blister on my foot and it's stinging a little.'

'Show me!' He came back close to the bed. 'Show me, Nella—or do you want me to throw back the cover and look for myself?'

Put like that, she had little option. Reluctantly she pushed down the duvet, glad that the nightdress came well below her knees as she offered her foot for his inspection.

'*Dios*!' He took her slender, pale foot in one hand, pursing his lips as he gazed down at the inflamed toe. 'You must have been in agony during the walk back to the car.'

'It was painful,' she admitted wryly. 'But preferable to the alternative.'

'Being carried back in my arms?' He raised a questioning eyebrow.

'Or being dragged back by my hair?' she queried, a spark of antagonism flaring in her amber eyes. 'Your mood at the time was hardly conducive to lending a sympathetic ear... or hand.'

'You think me cruel because I have moral values?' His face hardened imperceptibly. 'I am not totally without compassion, *mi cuñada*.'

There it was again, the deliberate repetition of her supposed relationship with him—sister-in-law—as if he was trying to stamp it in his mind.

Nella sighed. 'I supposed you would regard a mere blister as a minor punishment for the multitude of my sins,' she allowed ruefully, uncomfortably aware of his lean fingers encompassing her foot like a caress.

'You were wrong,' he informed her tersely. 'I would have regarded it as a wound with the potential to fester and would have bound it with a strip from my freshly laundered handkerchief.'

'Then I regret not informing you,' she said meekly. 'Is it too late to ask you to sacrifice your handkerchief now? I'm afraid I only have tissues with me.'

'I can do better than that. Stay where you are.' He released her foot and left the room. Nella stared down at her toes, the impression of his fingers lingering so powerfully that she half expected to see their prints on her instep. There was no evidence that he'd touched her, yet still the feeling of physical awareness persisted.

He was back in seconds, a packet of plasters in his hand.

'You travel well-prepared,' she said admiringly as he undid one and fastened it over the offending blister. 'It never occurred to me that you'd bring a medicine case with you.' She sighed her pleasure at the instant relief the covering afforded. There was something wonderfully satisfying about being tended to, in surrendering her hurt to someone else's ministration.

'That makes me a hypochondriac in your estimation?' he enquired drily. 'Let me disillusion you. My work in Venezuela often entails that I travel to remote areas of the country where medical attention is not near at hand. It's only prudent that I take precautions. A small first-aid pack has become an essential part of my luggage.'

'What do you do, then?' Curiosity prompted the question as Nella withdrew her foot beneath the safety of the all-encompassing duvet. 'You're not going to tell me that you're a missionary, are you?'

'Would it surprise you if I did?' He lifted his eyebrows at her as the lines at the side of his mobile mouth grooved into a half-smile. 'I suspect you already have me classified as some kind of zealot.'

He could read her mind! In her imagination he was St Peter at the gate to heaven, repelling all those who had not repented. 'Are you going to deny it?' she asked sweetly, aware of a strange kind of tension vibrating between the two of them as his amazing eyes regarded her through slightly lowered lids.

'No.' His reply was unqualified. 'When my heart's engaged I am a passionate man, and where my work is concerned it would be true to say I pursue it with whole-hearted zeal.'

'Let me guess.' The temptation to provoke him too strong to resist, Nella tilted her head to one side. 'You're some kind of tax collector?'

'Only where I am the creditor!' His teeth flashed in the brief, avaricious smile she was beginning to recognise as a precursor of battle. 'My company is engaged in the construction industry.'

'Oh, I see.' Nella nodded her head sagely. 'Apartments, hotels, corporate buildings—those kinds of things?'

'We've certainly been involved in some such projects.' A tinge of pride echoed in his voice. 'Caracas boasts some of the world's most beautiful and technologically advanced buildings, as well as a subway system of such excellence that it has become a tourist attraction.' He paused, the momentary arrogance subsiding as he continued, 'But there are other less glamorous buildings from which our country can benefit—for instance factories, especially in remote areas. Unfortunately, the importation of food and essential goods still imposes a heavy burden on our economy, and the exodus of people who cannot find employment where they live, and therefore make for the cities, poses enormous problems for the urban authorities.'

'You mean like the *favelas* of Brazil?' Fascinated to learn more, Nella gazed enquiringly into his animated face.

Raúl nodded. 'I see you know something about the problems.'

Was that a gleam of admiration she had surprised in his clear eyes? If it was he masked it quickly as he continued easily, 'In Venezuela we call the makeshift settlements *barrios*. On the road from La Guaira to Caracas you'll see hundreds of these temporary buildings clustered on the hills. Many of our critics refer to them as urban slums, but the people who choose to live there enjoy the same medical and educational facilities as the rest of our citizens. In fact, some of them come from less democratic regimes to find sanctuary and work. Obviously, theirs is not an ideal situation, but the alternatives are either to burn down the *barrios* and make them homeless or to increase the opportunities for employment outside the city areas.' He paused, then added, 'However, we don't deny or underestimate the situation. Our government has already developed alternative industries, mainly in the eastern part of the country, to encourage the spread of labour rather than allow it to be concentrated around the cities, but it's a slow process.'

'So you see yourself as a humanitarian as well as a businessman?'

'I see myself as a patriot,' he corrected coolly. 'Doing a worthwhile job to the best of my ability, and for a fair reward.'

'But not with your own hands?' Nella glanced at the hands which had so recently touched the tender skin of her foot. They were not the hands of a labourer.

'Not any more,' he admitted, a slight smile lifting the corners of his mouth. 'But given the necessity I could swing a shovel with the best of them, and a hard hat is no stranger to my head.'

Casting her gaze to rest on his strong, broad shoulders, Nella didn't doubt it. Raúl Farrington might be many things, but never effete. Finding it impossible to repress the small shudder which travelled down her spine as she recalled the hard virility of his body as it had encroached on her own only a few hours previously, she hastened to banish him from her room.

'Fascinating and instructive though I find your lecture on South American economics, Raúl, if you want me ready by nine I'd appreciate your continuing the lesson at a later date, because I'd like to get dressed.'

'Of course.' He gave her a courtly, rather old-fashioned half-bow from the waist, the expression on his face letting her know that his action was ironical. 'Don't forget to finish your tea, will you?'

He left, closing the door gently behind him.

It took Nella only a few seconds to empty her cup, grateful for the thirst-quenching properties of its contents. Slipping off the nightdress, she slid her nubile body into a featherlight bodyshaper before choosing one of the cotton dresses she'd packed—an exuberant print of hibiscus and tropical fruit. Low-necked and sleeveless, with a simply gathered skirt, it was ideal for the still warm temperature of the early evening. Whether it was elegant enough for the place he was taking her to was another matter. But, as Rosie had been fond of saying in the days before her affliction had shuttered her mind, it was manners that made a man—not the clothes he put on his back. If Raúl was ashamed of her appearance he'd have no one but himself to blame, by handing her his invitation at such short notice.

Thrusting her bare feet into her high-heeled sandals, she was delighted to find that their slender straps missed the plastered abrasion of her big toe. In the unlikely event of his asking her to dance, she'd see he wasn't disappointed!

Deciding to leave her hair loose for the evening, she brushed it back from her oval face, allowing it to fall in its own clinging volume to rest on her shoulderblades. Staring critically at herself in the mirror, she decided her face looked washed out above the vibrant cotton of the dress. An imp of mischief whispered in her ear. What kind of make-up would Luis's 'Nella' have put on for the evening? Something pretty outstanding, she guessed.

Humming off-key softly to herself, she got to work with her basic make-up kit, applying eye-shadow and eyeliner discreetly but to good effect. Carefully she darkened her lashes with two coats of mascara before outlining her soft, full-lipped mouth with a light scarlet lipstick which complemented the glowing colours of her dress. Lastly she reached for one of the atomisers with which her host had provided her, spraying the pulse-points at her neck and wrists lightly before examining herself critically in the long mirror.

She looked different—astonishingly different. She stared at her image, trying to see it through the eyes of someone else. For the first time in months she seemed alive, vibrant—in touch once more with hope and optimism after a period of mental and emotional imprisonment. And the man waiting for her downstairs had been the catalyst in her transformation.

Dear heavens! What had he done to her? He despised her for sins she'd never committed, held her in contempt as a liar and a thief, and yet for all that he had been the one to set her spirit free. His painful and misdirected barbs had shocked her out of her lethargy with all the efficiency of an electric probe. The aura of reserve which had cloaked her had finally begun to melt away and the old Nella, the bright, optimistic girl with a head full of ambitions and a love of life, had begun the journey to rebirth.

Raúl was waiting for her as she descended the staircase, his powerful yet elegant frame immaculately dressed in a silver-grey suit. There was a moment's uncomfortable silence as his eyes took their toll of her.

'Well?' she challenged boldly as the silence grew, painfully aware of her increased heartbeat and the flutter of the small pulse at her throat. 'Do I pass inspection or not?'

For a few seconds more he continued to stare at her, pinning her soft eyes, with their wealth of flaring, darkened lashes, with his own icily blue gaze, before saying softly, 'Oh, you pass, *querida*. How clever of you to choose such a simple dress as a foil to your beauty and to ignore the opportunity to bedeck your lovely skin with jewels. The result is understated but doubly enchanting.'

A backhanded compliment if ever she'd heard one! 'Your sarcasm does you no credit,' she retorted tartly. 'If I'd been aware this was an open prison I would have packed accordingly. If you're ashamed of me, then I'll stay here and you go without me.'

'You choose to misunderstand me.' Raúl laughed softly at the rebellious gleam in her eyes. 'Far from being ashamed of you, I intend to enjoy your company as far as propriety allows.' His gaze travelled over her beautifully made-up face, the clear, pale skin exposed in the lowered neckline of her dress. 'I can't wait to see the social skills which Luis found so captivating, and which persuaded him to wed you instead of just bedding you.' Then, before she could find an acid enough response to his insult, he was holding his hand out, lean and muscular tanned fingers reaching for her own, clasping their cool slenderness calmly to lead her towards the front door. 'Come, for tonight, at least, we shall have a truce.'

From outside the club had all the appearance of a country house set in extensive grounds. Everywhere the lighting was discreet, from the elegant foyer to the intimate bar and beyond, through sliding glass doors, to the garden, where a dozen or so tables were clustered around a circular wooden floor. Hooded lights at floor-level illuminated the small dance-floor, but beyond the main sources of illumination were long, flaring torches, artistically planted among a variety of shrubs, allied to the glow provided from individual candle-lamps placed on each table.

As a setting for a romantic interlude it couldn't be faulted, Nella acknowledged ruefully as she followed the head waiter across the dance-floor towards a table just outside the inner circle. The majority of tables were already occupied, mainly by couples, but two tables of four people caught her eye, as did a floorside table occupied by three young men whose casual attitude suggested they were *habitués* of the place.

It wasn't until she was seated that she noticed the canopied stand where two men, one seated behind a double keyboard and the other facing a formidable assembly of percussion instruments, were sorting through a pile of music.

'I trust this won't be too quiet for your tastes, Nella,' Raúl commented softly as the waiter handed her a menu and the music started.

'It seems idyllic.' Careful not to sound too ingenuous, she cast her eyes around, peering into the surrounding shadows. 'The kind of place to which important men

bring their mistresses.' The desire to tease him rose again,
unbidden. 'Is that how your contact discovered it, Raúl?'

'Probably,' he drawled. 'I see you are very worldly-
wise about these matters.'

'It would be difficult in today's society to remain
ignorant,' she commented drily, fluttering her eyelashes
at him seductively as she entered into the spirit of the
role she'd decided to play, and her body relaxed to the
rhythmic beat of the rumba which echoed through the
still night. 'Who is this benefactor? A relation, perhaps?'

'A friend.' Raúl's smile seemed extra white against
the tanned skin of his face. 'Someone I first met at
Oxford when I was studying there for two years in my
youth. Since then he's gained honours in many pres-
tigious fields, and despite our differences in race and
culture we have remained good friends even though our
meetings have been few and far between.' He paused
slightly before asking politely, 'Have you made your'
choice yet from the menu?'

Obviously he had no intention of discussing his friend
further, so Nella held her curiosity at bay, obediently
holding the menu towards the lamplight, the better to
read its elegant scrawl.

She hadn't felt hungry, but since Raúl had assured her
she could take her time, she'd ordered cucumber *por-
tugaise*, followed by turbot *au four* served with broccoli
spears and creamed potatoes. Surprisingly, when she'd
finished the last delicious piece of turbot, she found
herself tempted—probably due to the several glasses of
Pouilly-Fuissé which had accompanied the main meal—
to order a dessert, finally allowing herself to be persuaded by Raúl to sample the strawberries Romanov.

'Will you excuse me a moment, please?' Raúl rose
courteously to his feet as she toyed with the last re-

maining strawberries in their bed of portwine and cream.
'I've just seen someone I have to speak to.'

Nodding her agreement, Nella watched him skirt round
the outside of the dance-floor and disappear into the
shadows, leaving her with an ideal opportunity to visit
the ladies' room and repair her make-up.

The elegant powder-room was deserted as she gazed
uncertainly at her own reflection in the mirror. Her
cheeks were flushed, her eyes sparkling. Hesitantly she
touched her glowing skin, unable to believe the metamorphosis which had taken place in her appearance. It
was as if she'd finally made a break with the past. The
face which stared back at her was that of the carefree
Nella, before the responsibilities of caring for Rosie had
sucked her spirit dry.

It was a heady realisation which lent wings to her feet
as, having repaired her lipstick, she started back towards
the garden, where the musicians had just begun to play
a lively version of "Ain't Misbehavin'". Crossing the
empty dance-floor *en route* to her table, she saw that
Raúl had not yet returned to it. Before she'd even realised
what she was doing, she'd paced her walk to the beat of
the music and executed a tiny sequence of tap-dance steps
in perfect accord with it.

It would have ended there if she hadn't received a small
ripple of applause from the three young men she'd
noticed earlier. Their approval was flattering; so much
so that, tossing them an appreciative smile, she added
a few more steps. An appreciative cry of 'Yes!' from
the musician on percussion was the final incentive she
needed. As the tempo increased to tempt her she matched
it, moving gracefully towards her final destination, her
heels clicking with the precision of castanets as she
swayed across the floor. It was all over in seconds, re-

warded by smiles from people on the surrounding tables and an elegant and sweeping bow from one of the young men who had originally encouraged her.

'How right you were, Nella. Your skill for dancing is certainly still alive and kicking.' Raúl's softly spoken words ate into her euphoria like acid etching a zinc plate as the musicians, picking up the mood of their audience, launched into a spirited rendering of "Masks and Faces".

# CHAPTER EIGHT

SWIRLING round, Nella found him confronting her, his hands gripping the back of her empty chair.

'You were watching? I didn't see you...' she began, discomfited by the glowering frown directed at her and instantly regretting her untypical display of light-heartedness.

'A circumstance for which I'm delighted.' His teeth showed whitely in a smile totally devoid of humour. 'Because from your demeanour at dinner I was finding it difficult to believe that you were the high-spirited exhibitionist Luis described so fulsomely to me.'

Nella felt her temper rise. She'd been about to apologise if her little dance had embarrassed him, but she'd done nothing to deserve this scathing assessment. 'Perhaps you should consider yourself lucky I didn't decide to do a striptease!' she challenged furiously, moving her head with an arrogant toss which sent her hair swirling about her shoulders.

He stiffened as though she'd struck him. 'No, *querida*,' he said between gritted teeth, his glare burning through her. 'It is *you* who should be grateful that you decided to show a modicum of restraint. But since you enjoy being the cynosure of all attention...' With one lithe movement he shrugged his jacket from his shoulders and slung it across the back of his chair.

'For pity's sake, Raúl!' Shock wiped the defiance from Nella's face as she teetered away from his vengeful countenance, her imagination conjuring up images of humiliating retribution.

'Too late for pity, Nella!' He caught her hand, drawing her body hard against his own. 'After such a delightful display of talent, you'll never convince me you can't dance a tango.'

Tango? Relief and despair mingled as he pulled her on to the floor to join two other couples already there. She knew the basic steps and nothing more, but ignorance was not about to spare her. As Raúl's powerful body commanded her movement she found herself with no option but to follow his lead.

She'd known from the beginning that it was to be no polite tea-dance tango, but even then she hadn't anticipated that it would turn into a savage exhibition that screamed of its origin in the brothels of Argentina. She was angry and dishevelled at first, as Raúl bent her body to his command, forcing her into exaggerated postures, the warmth of his skin overwhelming her as it burned through the fine shirt which clung tightly to his muscled chest, but by the time the other couples had retired to the edge of the dance-floor, denied the space to compete, she was matching him move for move, hair flying, lips parted as hard-faced and unsmiling he thrust her round the floor.

Gasping for breath, she clung weakly to him as the final chords climaxed into silence as he bent her backwards across his arm, his thigh a brutal intruder between her legs, his mouth imprisoning hers with a passionate, brutal kiss as spontaneous applause splattered into the warm, still air.

'Satisfied?' He was breathing heavily as he dragged her off the floor. 'Is that enough acclaim to make you happy? To arouse you?' He pulled his coat off the chair, thrusting his arms into it. 'Or shall I ask the band to let you sing with them?' His eyes met hers disparagingly.

'I want to leave.' She was shaking, her lips throbbing where his mouth had burned its message of contempt.

'So do I,' he muttered thickly. 'What an apt title, hmm? "Masks and Faces." How many other masks have graced that lovely face, I wonder, in your career of deception?'

'How dare you kiss me...?' Her voice breaking, she pursued her own vendetta. He was too experienced, too practised not to have realised just how much his public seduction had aroused her—and he had not been un- moved by her proximity either. She'd sensed the physical torment raging within him, and had been both excited and intrigued by it at the time, momentarily forgetting that he believed she was his brother's wife. Now she saw in his eyes only the reflection of the degradation to which he'd submitted her.

'I dared because your eyes invited me, your body tempted me...' His profile was rigid as he turned away from her to wave an imperious credit card in the di- rection of a passing waiter. 'I dared because both of us know that Luis can never be the husband you either need or deserve!'

The evening had ended in total disaster, and she'd had no one but herself to blame. It was one thing to vent her irritation with Raúl by refusing to continue vainly protesting her innocence, quite another to allow herself to enter too dramatically into the role she'd been allo- cated. The silent journey back to the cottage in an at- mosphere so hostile that she hadn't even dared to utter a further word of well-earned rebuke, had been chas- tening enough.

Wearily Nella slid her nightdress over her head as she prepared for bed. Even worse was the knowledge that perhaps, after all, she did have something in common with that other Nella—a lust for life which she had only just discovered...

As the cool sheets received her tired body she curled herself into the foetal position. Worst of all was the realisation that Raúl's devastating performance on the dance-floor had awakened feelings and emotions she'd never known before. Competent but not expert, her dancing ability hadn't mattered as Raúl had bent her entirely to his will—taking, leading, educating. It had been a breathless lesson in more ways than one.

For so many years it had seemed as if she was the person in charge, and it had been a responsibility she'd been glad to accept. Now, frighteningly, she felt a deep need to yield some of her autonomy, to lean on Raúl's obvious strength, to let him support her emotionally as he had physically that night.

She shuddered. How much worse it would have been if, at that last exciting climax, he had withdrawn his arm and let her fall abandoned to the floor! He had spared her then. On another occasion he probably wouldn't... There must never be another occasion...

It seemed hours before sleep claimed her, as her over-pitched nervous system refused to relax. Then, when sleep eventually came, she found herself pitched into a maelstrom of troubled dreams.

It was a rapid and impatient series of knocks on her bedroom door which awakened her at the very moment when it seemed she might have found peace.

'Yes, yes . . .' She shot upright in bed, blinking in the bright sunlight which filled the room, trying to orientate her thoughts. 'What is it? What's happening?'

'Not daybreak, for sure!' Raúl thrust himself into the room, presumably taking her questions as permission to do so. 'That happened many hours ago.' He passed a quick, all-encompassing glance over her face. 'There are things to be done today, so I'm afraid you'll have to settle for the beauty sleep you've already enjoyed.'

'What things?' she demanded suspiciously, her mouth dry, her mind still drugged by the remnants of sleep as she tried to read his mood.

'We have to go to Salisbury,' he returned briskly. 'Unfortunately, because of your defection and his subsequent accident, Luis was unable to complete his business. So I've undertaken to make the last few calls outstanding on his behalf. Naturally, you'll be coming with me.'

Nella stared back at his autocratic face, shocked by what she saw as his uninterest in his brother's welfare. 'You're going to leave Luis alone in hospital while you go on tour of the country?' she asked, amazed. 'Shouldn't you be nearby to comfort him when he regains consciousness?'

'Unnecessary,' he returned succinctly. 'Because he'll find his mother and his aunt sitting at his bedside. My mother and her sister arrived from Caracas earlier today and were met by a good friend from the consulate. He took them to the best hotel in Exeter, where they will want for nothing, and has arranged for all their needs to be met, at my expense.'

'But——' Nella began to protest.

'But nothing!' he interposed firmly. 'Be assured that Mamá will provide him with all the love and sympathy he needs—in abundance—and, since I deliberately re-frained from informing her of his unsuitable alliance, I intend to keep you as far away as possible from both of them. My mother, who was widowed two years ago, has enough trauma to contend with in coming to terms with the fact that she nearly lost her younger, most beloved son, without having an unexpected, unwanted and im-moral daughter-in-law thrust on her!'

He glanced down at his watch. 'Oh, and in case you're interested, your husband spent a restful night and the hospital is optimistic that his periods of consciousness will be extended. Now, if you can bring yourself to face the day, I'd like to leave within the hour.'

As changes of plans went, this one was probably for the better, she decided fifty-five minutes later, obediently handing over her small suitcase to be stowed away in the Jaguar's boot.

Taking her place in the passenger seat and fastening her seatbelt as Raúl eased his athletically built body behind the driving-wheel, she found her mind returning to the previous night's dreams. The memory brought a blush to mantle her cheeks. Dear heavens! What strange magic had this arrogant stranger at her side wrought over her that she should enjoy such fantasies as those which had plagued her during the small dark hours? Raúl, stripped and beautiful, on his knees at her feet . . . Raúl, persuasive and penitent, begging her forgiveness for ever doubting her veracity. . . Raúl, proud and dominant, poised to possess her as she opened her body to welcome him . . . Raúl . . .

'Why not open the window if you find the heat op-pressive?' his gentle voice suggested. 'If I'd known the weather would be so hot I would have hired a convertible.'

Glad to turn sideways, so that her flushed cheeks were hidden from him, Nella complied, cursing her pale skin which betrayed every surge of adrenalin which flowed through her bloodstream. Was it possible he had divined her thoughts—or had he genuinely put down her increased colour to the warmth inside the car? For her own peace of mind she must assume the latter.

'So...tell me more about your grandmother.' His voice broke into her embarrassed thoughts.

'Rosie?'

'Unless your other grandmother played a large role in your early life?'

'She didn't.' Nella cast him a rebuking glance, which he appeared not to notice. 'In fact, she died before I was born.'

'Rosie, then,' he agreed smoothly. 'You can start by telling me why you called her by that name. Is it normal in this country to address one's senior relatives by their Christian names?'

'I imagine it depends on the relatives,' Nella informed him coolly, aware of the implied criticism in his remark. 'My grandmother's name was Eliza Rosina, but she always liked to be called Rosie. She was such a fun person—pretty, full of life, generous... Ageless... until she became ill.' She paused, feeling the tears of frustration filling her eyes.

'And you cared for her for two years—until she died?'

'Yes.' Her reply was curt, the ache in her throat too great to make speaking easy.

'It wasn't possible to get her into a hospital? Or some kind of home?' Raúl's cool persistence into matters she'd prefer to forget made Nella's temper rise.

'Oh, yes, it was possible,' she retorted heatedly. 'In fact Michael, her doctor that was, suggested it. He told me I was sacrificing my whole future by devoting myself to her when there was no hope for improvement. But when you love someone it's not so easy to abandon them.'

Too late, she realised the trap into which she'd unwittingly fallen.

'Exactly!' Raúl hissed. 'Despite the fact that Luis was completely bowled over by your beauty, you never felt even the slightest bit of affection for him, did you?' To her relief the question appeared to be rhetorical as he continued brutally, '*Dios*! How eloquent your body must have been to persuade him to offer you his name. Tell me, Nella, was it always his money you were after or were you seeking someone to love you? Someone to replace your grandmother's lost affection? Someone who would shoulder the kind of responsibilities you'd taken on and which had perhaps proved too much for you?'

'Is that what you believe, Raúl?' She offered him the kind of smile she imagined her impersonator might have proferred in the circumstances. 'I didn't realise you were a psychology graduate. Are you trying to find excuses for me?'

'Reasons, perhaps,' he muttered, barely audibly. 'It must have been flattering to have been made the centre of his attention. Perhaps you meant well at the beginning—then, when he had to leave you temporarily to go about his business, you realised his money could bring you more happiness and fulfilment than his immature love.'

Nella didn't answer, but she allowed her gaze to rest on his countenance, observing the effect on it of his thought-processes. 'Or,' he continued after a short pause, 'were you being manipulated by someone else, hmm? A man, perhaps? Someone whom you really did care for, but who was looking for a woman with money to satisfy his own ambitions? Am I right, Nella? Is that how it happened?'

She forced herself to laugh, a light, breathy sound lacking sincerity, as the ache in her heart deepened in response to his overt scorn. 'As a psychoanalyst you make a good engineer,' she quipped, deliberately facetious. 'Don't throw away the hard hat.'

'Very amusing!' He applauded her wit by giving her a flashing smile, but the bright sparkle of his blue eyes was cold and scathing as it washed over her provocatively held face. 'But don't make the mistake of trying to dismiss me too easily. Cleverer opponents than you have learned to their dismay that I make a bad enemy.'

He lapsed into silence, much to Nella's relief. Left to her own devices, she began to search her memory of events over the past few weeks for any incontrovertible proof that whoever the woman with Luis had been, it hadn't been her! But until she knew where she was *supposed* to have been, she could hardly prove that she hadn't been there! She could almost feel sorry for Luis's real wife, blissfully unaware of the threats of vengeance awaiting her!

She sighed wearily. Time. It was just a matter of time. All she had to do was relax and try not to antagonise the man who had precipitated himself into her life and temporarily taken charge of it. In the meantime, she would look forward to visiting the beautiful city of Salisbury with its renowned cathedral which, if she remembered correctly, had an entrance for every month of the year, a window for every day and a column for every hour as well as the highest spire in England.

The mood of depression which had overcome her during the brief acrimonious exchange with Raúl lifted. He wouldn't want to take her with him on his business visits, and it was hardly likely that he intended to lock her up in the bedroom of the hotel into which he'd assured her he'd booked them, so presumably she would have time to explore.

'Mr and Mrs Farrington?'

The receptionist simpered up into Raúl's aggressively handsome face. 'Room 304. The porter will bring your luggage up in a few minutes.' She handed Raúl a key attached to a sizeable onyx label. 'Enjoy your stay.'

'I'm sure we shall.' Tucking his hand firmly beneath Nella's elbow, he propelled her in the direction of the lift.

'What the blazes do you think you're playing at?' Furiously she rounded on him as soon as the doors had closed behind them on the otherwise empty lift. 'How dare you book us in as husband and wife? I haven't the slightest intention of sharing a room with you.'

'*Paz, querida*!' He held both hands up in mock despair. 'Consider my situation. Do you think I wish to spend the night with a virago—and one, moreover, who is bound to my own brother? When I phoned for accommodation I asked for two rooms, but only one was vacant. Since it was a large double I agreed to take it. I assure you I made no claim to be your husband. I merely gave them your name. However, I would have thought in the circumstances it would be more fitting if they made the incorrect assumption that we are man and wife.'

'It would have been more fitting if you'd found another hotel for me,' Nella returned grimly.

'And leave you to your own resources all night?' He slanted quizzical eyebrows at her as his lips curled derisively. 'What kind of fool do you take me for, Rusty? I've no intention of going on a wild-goose chase all over the city, searching the public houses for you. Neither do I mean to allow you to pick up any more unfortunates who are slightly the worse for indulging in drink and use your wiles on them.'

'Like I did on Luis, you mean?'

The lift-gates had opened and Raúl was marching her down a long corridor with such determined strides that she had to run to keep up with him.

'Precisely!' he agreed brutally. 'I brought you with me not because I wanted to enjoy your company but because, as I've explained, it was the lesser of two evils. But be warned, I intend to do everything in my power to ensure you behave yourself with dignity, as befits my sister-in-law.'

'And that includes sharing your bedroom?' Nella enquired, raising her eyebrows and fluttering her long lashes at him with deliberate provocation which hid her anger. 'I only hope Luis will understand the situation.'

'Depend on it, I will make sure he does.' They'd arrived at Room 304 and Raúl's promise was accompanied by a sharp movement of his arm as he thrust Nella across its threshold. 'There, you see!' he exclaimed in triumph. 'You can't complain at that.'

Couldn't she? Nella's eyes made a quick inventory of the large room. Writing-desk, two easy chairs, fitted wardrobe, ample cupboard room, mirror and two double beds separated by a substantial bedside table, the latter bearing a vase of dark red roses, the perfume and velvety texture of which she recognised as being that of the variety Josephine Bruce—one of her favourites.

Luxurious, she had to admit. All the same, she'd never shared a room with a man in her life, and the intimacy of such an arrangement held no appeal for her. Particularly when the man in question was Raúl Farrington.

'I don't like it,' she said flatly.

'Then you'll just have to put up with it, Rusty,' he retorted firmly. 'Because this is how it's going to be.'

'Why have you suddenly started calling me Rusty?' She regarded him belligerently, momentarily distracted from the problem of a bed for the night.

'Because it suits you.' His blue eyes narrowed to slits as he reached to take a handful of hair in his palm. 'Your hair is what we call *oxidado*, no?'

'Oh.' She moved away, frowning, and he let her go. 'Frankly I prefer to think of it as russet rather than rusty, and I'd prefer to be called by my proper name, if you don't mind. But, regardless of what you call me, it won't change my mind about not sharing a room with you.'

'As you wish.' He shrugged. 'I wonder what the papers will make of David Lambert's sister signing in at a Salisbury hotel under the name of Mrs Farrington? Especially when the full story of her deception comes out.'

'I wonder what Señora Farrington will make of her elder son being discovered in the same bedroom as her younger son's wife?' Nella retorted wildly, infuriated by his calmness and frustrated by the implicit threat.

He laughed. 'Very little, since she cannot read English.'

'Very well,' Nella capitulated ungraciously. 'Rather than risk prejudicing David's chances of election, I agree to share the room. I just hope you don't snore.'

'You'll have to advise me about that in the morning.' He sat down on one of the beds, testing the springs. 'Fortunately I have no such doubts about you. According to my brother you were like an angel in his arms all night...' He paused to survey her thoughtfully. 'Myself—I prefer a devil.'

It was perhaps as well that the porter delivered their cases at that moment, somewhat defusing the situation. She was being absurd to allow him to rile her, Nella lectured herself silently as she unpacked. Why, oh, why, was she harbouring these strange, jumbled-up emotions about a man who despised her? A stranger who considered her a thief as well as a seductress and regarded her with barely veiled contempt. Yesterday, by the boulder beach, he'd tricked her in the most despicable way and, innocent fool that she was, she'd fallen for his applied charm.

Unconscious of the action, she ran her tongue round her lips, remembering the taste and touch of his hard mouth on her own. Her heightened senses responding to memory, she swayed slightly as she recalled the power of his body against her own, a terrible fear filtering through into her consciousness. If she hadn't called a halt would Raúl have taken her body and then denounced her to his brother as the *ramera* he had labelled her?

She shuddered, escaping to the bathroom to hang up her sponge-bag and to avoid the steady regard of his perceptive eyes. Like it or not, she was forced to recognise that there was a chemistry between them—disruptive, dangerous and potentially destructive. She didn't like it. Why, then, was she reacting to it? Flirting with the kind of volatility which could explode in her face?

Perhaps over the past years her will-power had been weakened, her instinct for self-preservation diminished, her ability to judge warped? Because the bitter truth was that despite everything he'd done to her, and said about her, Raúl Farrington had won her grudging admiration, and something else which she was loath to dignify with the name of love, but for which she could find no other title. It was as if, beneath the hard shell of his hostility, she had sensed the presence of a tender, compassionate soul, reaching out towards her at a subliminal level. She shook her head in an effort to dispel the rogue thought.

'So what's the programme?' she demanded unemotionally, after having refreshed her hands and face. 'Do you intend to shackle me to your side while you make your business calls?'

'An interesting hypothesis.' He swept an assessing scrutiny over her contentious face. 'I can think of worse fates than being shackled to a beautiful woman, but I suspect my English hosts are more conservative and would find the prospect somewhat disturbing.' He flashed her a swift, superior smile. 'So I've decided to put my trust in your sense of self-preservation and your need to keep your brother's loyalty in respect of any future negotiations, and leave you to your own devices until lunchtime.'

'Wow! Lucky me!' Nella's hazel eyes flashed with unusual acrimony, targeting on the thick glossy hair at the back of his head as he turned away from her to place some of his clothes in a drawer. Not only did she resent the derogatory tone in which he'd addressed her but she suspected the girl who had married Luis would have resented it even more. She threw caution to the winds, adding for good measure, 'Would you like me to show my gratitude by genuflecting and kissing your hand?'

The moment she'd spoken she sensed she'd gone too far, stepping back swiftly as Raúl swivelled on his heel.

'*Ten cuidado, querida*!' He approached her with such swiftness that no escape was left open to her as his hand seized her shoulder. 'One day you will twist the jaguar's tail too often and too hard and be forced to bear the consequences of your rash action.'

'You're threatening to maul me?' Her heart was thundering like the feet of a stampeding herd, but there was a heady excitement in teasing him, knowing the powerful constraints which bound him to treat her with respect. 'Wouldn't you find that difficult to explain to Luis?'

His hand tightened on her shoulder, the fingers pressing into the bone with warning pressure. 'Luis may not always be your protector,' he told her harshly.

'Amen,' she breathed with a heartfelt sigh, then immediately regretted her instinctive reaction as she heard the hiss of his intake of breath.

'Ah, but then I, as head of the family, will take over his right for vengeance, *guapa*,' he told her softly. 'And I am not as easily fooled or as forgiving as my brother.'

'I'm trembling with fear!' Nella forced her lips into a smile, which did nothing to conceal the fact that she *was* actually trembling. Fear had been her excuse, but she recognised instinctively that the adrenalin which had flooded her bloodstream at his nearness and the soft, intimate promise of his voice had nothing to do with fear.

'So I see.' Raúl's enigmatic gaze played on the slight, uncontrollable movement of her lips, and it was all she could do not to moisten them with her tongue, some inner caution warning her against such a provocative action. '*Dios*! But women such as you should be kept under strict control,' he informed her tautly. 'Instead of being let loose to wreak your charms on innocent youths.'

'Among which you include yourself?' Nella raised an enquiring eyebrow, allowing the corners of her mouth to curve upwards into a challenging smile as something

alien in her nature drove her to taunt him rather than
to subside beneath his contempt.

'Come, now, you know better than that, *guapa*!'
Raúl's voice was thick as he addressed her softly. 'I shan't
be seeing thirty again, and as for innocence—I lost that
before my twentieth birthday.'

'Not till then?' she mocked him, riding on the exhila-
rating tide of hormones which sang in her blood. 'That
seems a little late by present-day standards.'

'But then I'm a selective predator,' he returned without
a pause. 'Not for me the willing women who throw
themselves in my path. I seek only the hard to find, the
near impossible to possess. So, tell me, where in your
wide-ranging and early-begun experience did Luis come,
hmm? Was he among the lovers you can count on one
hand?'

Nella swallowed, felt her eyelashes flutter in confusion, angry with herself for setting herself up.

'No?' He took her silence for denial. 'Two hands,
then?'

'No...' The word stuck in her throat as her confidence suddenly drained. 'No,' she repeated more firmly.
'Luis and I...' She paused, unwilling to deny the relationship which, for all its falsity, was her strongest
protection against the potent sensuality of the man whose
present nearness was having strangely intoxicating ef-
fects on her senses.

'What are you trying to say, Nella?' His voice was
oddly gentle now, as he took her slim, cool hand in his
own. 'Not that Luis was your first lover, surely?'

'No,' she agreed faintly, grasping the opportunity of
telling the truth without weakening her security. She gave
a little choking laugh which mocked herself, not the
question, her eyes closing briefly as she tried to imagine

the expression on Raúl's face if she told him the truth—
that until he, Raúl, had entered her life she had never
felt the slightest desire to relinquish her virginity to any
man. 'No, he wasn't my first lover.'

He dropped her hand and moved away as Nella's legs
suddenly weakened and she sat down thankfully on the
edge of the bed, forcing herself to face the implication
of her own realisation. It hadn't been an illusion. She
was in love with this fiery, vengeful Venezuelan who
considered her lower than the dirt beneath his feet!

'You can amuse yourself as you wish for what's left
of the morning.' His voice was expressionless as he lifted
his briefcase on to the dressing-table and began to sort
through some papers. 'I'll meet you in the bar at one
o'clock. Please don't keep me waiting.'

'Fine by me.' Still shocked by the realisation of her
feelings, Nella would have agreed readily to any plan he
proposed. 'Isn't tourism rather a change of career direction for you?' she added, addressing his formidable
back. 'I mean, it's hardly what you've been trained for,
is it?'

Strong shoulders shrugged negligently beneath the
lightweight fawn fabric of his suit jacket. 'The ability
to sell is not necessarily confined to one pursuit or
practice...or person. As you, as much as anyone, should
be aware, Nella,' he told her, his tone softly incisive.
'Sometimes in this life it is necessary to court more than
one suitor, no?'

He didn't wait for her answer, presumably taking her
agreement for granted as he snapped the briefcase
closed, before striding from the room without a
backward glance.

# CHAPTER NINE

HEAVING a sigh of heartfelt relief as the door clicked
firmly shut behind Raúl's retreating back, Nella subsided thankfully on the bed. For the first time since his
unexpected arrival in her life she'd been left to her own
devices, and the feeling was a heady one.

A glance at her watch told her there was too little time
before lunch to indulge in any serious exploration of the
town, but the hotel itself was attractive enough to keep
her occupied until Raúl returned. She'd glimpsed an
arcade of stylish shops as they'd entered the foyer, and
a notice pointing to the gardens and swimming-pool.
What could be more pleasant than relaxing in the shade
by the pool and reading a paperback?

Seconds later she was making her way to the arcade,
passing an imposing staircase which pointed out the direction of conference rooms and a lecture theatre. Beneath it an ornately drawn card welcomed delegates to
a medical lecture on care for geriatrics in the community, and to the marketing representatives of a large
toy manufacturer. Since some of the delegates would
doubtless be staying overnight, perhaps Raúl had been
telling her the truth after all, she thought a trifle guiltily,
when he'd told her that theirs had been the last room
available.

The bookshop held a large and varied selection of
fiction, but somehow nothing attracted her. After all,
what kind of fiction could begin to compare with the
strange situation in which she found herself? What she

needed was something in which to immerse her mind—
something entertaining but factual. She found it in a
volume of logic puzzles, and was on her way towards
the pool when she saw the flame crepon sundress in a
small boutique.

An odd combination of simplicity and seductiveness,
its beautifully shaped bodice was surmounted by shoe-
string straps and its flared skirt sported a deep flounce.
She stopped, entranced. Not a dress for Nella Lambert,
but a creation that Nella Farrington would have delighted in wearing, realising that the eye-catching combination of dress and hair would bring her admiring
glances.

It was expensive, but since she'd recently received her
half-share of Rosie's cottage it was something she could
well afford. Ten minutes later she was walking out of
the shop, the stylish bag containing her prize beneath
her arm, her plans already made. An hour's relaxation
beside the pool, exercising her powers of reasoning, then
back to the room to assume the outward appearance of
the voluptuous, irresistible Nella Farrington!

She entered the crowded bar fifteen minutes early,
swaying across the room in her high-heeled sandals and
perching herself on one of the high stools against the
counter. Once she wouldn't have noticed the glances of
admiration tossed in her direction by the mainly male
occupants, now she found a quiet amusement in being
their recipient.

'Geriatrics or toys?' A middle-aged man cast her a
pleasant smile. 'And, whichever it is, can I buy you a
drink?'

'Actually, it's neither,' Nella confessed with a smile.
'And I'm expecting to meet someone here.'

'Lucky guy!' He nodded understandingly. 'I guess he wouldn't appreciate you being someone else's guest?'

'Afraid not,' Nella returned cheerfully.

'Dr Michael Wheatley... Dr Michael Wheatley... Telephone call for Dr Michael Wheatley...' A disembodied voice sounded above the general clamour of the bar.

Michael Wheatley? Nella swung round on her stool. Surely not *her* Michael? Rosie's doctor who had been so kind to her? The man who had actually asked her to be his wife? No, that would be too much of a coincidence... and it was hardly an uncommon name. Yet— community care for geriatrics... That had been one of Michael's main interests...

Then she saw him, easing his way through the crowd towards the bar.

'I'm Michael Wheatley——' Then he saw her and stopped still. 'Nella! How wonderful! Good grief! What a surprise to see you here. Are you one of the delegates?'

'Michael! It's marvellous to see you again!' He'd opened his arms to her and impulsively she entered them, returning his hug. 'No, I'm here independently, with...with a friend.' Unexpectedly she felt a surge of blood rise to her cheeks. How on earth could she explain Raúl Farrington's true role in her life to Michael without appearing demented? 'Shouldn't you answer your phone call?' she asked breathlessly, indicating the telephone which had been placed on the bar for his use.

'Oh, right...yes.' He picked up the receiver. 'Wheatley speaking.' He shook his head as he replaced it. 'No one there. Couldn't have been important.' He regarded Nella's face thoughtfully. 'Do I take it you're lunching with this—er—friend?' he asked perceptively, 'And that in the circumstances, it might be a little embarrassing if we started discussing old times right now?'

'It could be,' she admitted ruefully. 'Raúl does tend to exercise a rather outdated macho proprietorship over me.'

'Very understandable!' Michael's eyes showed his appreciation. 'You were always lovely, Nella, but now you're absolutely beautiful. You can't imagine how delighted I am to see you so completely recovered from the trauma you suffered looking after Rosie. There are so many questions I'd like to ask you, but the last thing I want to do is create trouble...' He turned as if to go.

'No, wait, Michael!' Nella grabbed his arm. 'I'm not going to let you escape like that! I want to know what you're doing now. If you're still living in Lowdale Heath...' She gave an exasperated sigh, unwilling to expose this gentle and compassionate man to Raúl's particular brand of cynicism. 'Look, perhaps we could meet somewhere after lunch?' she suggested brightly. 'Raúl has another appointment this afternoon. I could meet you in the foyer after he's left? Unless you've got another lecture...' Her voice tailed away enquiringly.

Michael grinned, his pleasant face becoming even more attractive. 'The old Nella would never have dreamed of being so devious.' He gave her arm a squeeze. 'I'm delighted to tell you that I don't have to sign in again until half-past four. That should give us plenty of time to catch up on our news. When you're ready, you'll find me sitting in the foyer waiting for you.' He gave her a conspiratorial smile and a wink before losing himself in the crowd.

It was a few minutes to one. Anxiously Nella turned her gaze towards the entrance and was rewarded by seeing Raúl's dark head as he wove his way towards her.

'I'm sorry if I kept you waiting.' He offered the apology as a formality.

'I've only just arrived myself,' she lied brightly. 'Did you have a successful morning?'

'Very much so,' he informed her tersely, continuing smoothly, with just a hint of irritation apparent in his silky voice, 'Shall we continue this conversation over lunch? I have no wish to be late for my afternoon appointment.'

'Of course,' she agreed demurely. 'Your wish is my command.'

'Let's hope I don't have recourse to remind you of that statement.' He took her arm firmly, escorting her towards the dining-room with a positive stride that had the cluster of guests assembled there parting like hair beneath the application of a steel comb to allow them unhindered progress.

Light blue mesmeric eyes drank in her altered appearance as Nella sank gratefully on to the comfortable dining-chair the waiter had pulled out for her.

'So, how did you spend the morning?' It was a smoothly posed question as Raúl appeared to concentrate on the extensive menu, but Nella wasn't deceived by it, the delicate antennae of her perception sensing that in some way it was a test. Besides, she had no need to lie—or at least only partially.

'Shopping, lazing around the pool...'

'Mmm, much as I anticipated.' He leant across the table, his beautiful eyes taunting her. 'Have you decided what you want? What you wish to eat, I mean.'

Of course, she thought, he expected her to relay her wishes to him and he would convey them on her behalf. An old-fashioned courtesy which was seldom put into practice nowadays, when women preferred to discuss their choice direct with the waiter. Even though she realised that many women felt there was an element of patronage implicit in the custom, it was something she, personally, couldn't get aroused over.

In fact, she decided, there was something rather pleasing about being regarded as Raúl Farrington's protégée. Love him or hate him—and most of the time she couldn't differentiate between those two emotions where he was concerned—there was no doubt that he possessed an aura in which authority and intellect merged to make him outstanding among his peers. Somehow she found the warmth of his reflected glory provided an atmosphere in which her own personality could blossom— if only he were to encourage it a little...

'No starter,' she told him coolly, disciplining her mind to return to the present. 'Just the cold salmon salad.'

'And wine?'

'A good Chablis?' she suggested, confident in her choice but hardly able to suppress her surprise when, several minutes later, the wine waiter having produced a bottle and shown the label to Raúl, the latter indicated the *she* should go through the ritual of sampling and approving it. 'Lovely.' She savoured the bouquet before tasting and gave her verdict with a smile, conscious all the time of her companion's steady regard.

'What a complex woman you are, Nella.' He waited until their main course had been served and the waiter had left the table before breaking the silence. 'The more I see of you the more confused I become by the mixture of seeming innocence and sophistication in your personality.' He lifted his glass and took a mouthful of wine. 'Perhaps you've missed a vocation as an actress, hmm?'

'Perhaps,' she agreed placatingly.

'So what part are you auditioning for this afternoon?' Raúl's question sent a tremor of uncertainty through her nervous system.

'I don't understand.' She opened her eyes wide and tried to look innocent, but her heart was pounding beneath the thin covering of the sundress. Surely he had no knowledge of her forthcoming innocent tryst with Michael?

'The change of dress,' he prompted her, his eyes lingering on the bright bodice. 'What role do you see yourself in now—the gypsy temptress?'

She swallowed uncertainly, uncomfortable beneath the shuttered scrutiny of his gimlet eyes. 'I don't understand. Whom should I be trying to tempt?'

'That's what worries me,' he confessed silkily. 'But something has happened since I left you this morning. Someone or something has put a sparkle in your eyes and quickened your step. Some barely controlled emotion has brought a flush to your cheeks and a dewy freshness to your mouth.'

'I had a slight headache earlier. Now it's gone and I feel brighter.' Lightly Nella tried to dismiss the truth of his observations. 'Whatever else could there be?' She bent her head to concentrate on her salmon.

'Well, there could always be me.' The softly voiced startling suggestion brought the colour flooding to her cheeks. 'Is it, Nella? Am I supposed to be so impressed by your red-haired beauty and your flaunting skirts that I shall be prepared to deal more leniently with you? Find excuses for the way you deceived Luis? Become the arbitrator between you instead of one of the chief prosecutors?'

'You're being absurd!' Her whole body glowed beneath his steady appraisal and her ears sang, astonished by the double-edged compliments spelt out in his deep, honeyed voice. They were surrounded by other lunchers, but they could have been alone as far as the impact of his words on her battered emotions was concerned. With a sickening lurch of her solar plexus, Nella recognised the sexual tension thrumming between them for what it was.

His mind and body locked in conflict, Raúl found her physically attractive, and hated himself for his own weakness. Unfortunately it was she who was going to be burdened with the blame for unconsciously inflaming his senses. She'd been aware of him as a virile hunting male from the moment he'd burst into her life, and the confusion of their situation had done nothing to enable her to pretend otherwise. Oh, yes, she'd tried. But to a master of the game like Raúl her attempts at concealment must have been pathetic. The irony was that had she been the experienced seductress he believed her, she would never have been so vulnerable to his brutal charm.

'Absurd, am I?' He leaned towards her across the table. 'Then tell me why you found it necessary to change your dress? Tell me what magic elixir has made you incandescent?'

With an effort she controlled her jangling nerves, keeping her voice low so as not to be overheard. 'Why do people change their clothes? Because they're travel-worn, of course. Tell me——' she carried the war into his own camp '—what is it about my dress that offends you?'

'Offends?' He laughed softly. 'On the contrary, I find it enchanting—captivating, even. Too vibrantly attractive to be confined to the walls of a hotel bedroom—or do you have other plans for this afternoon?'

His eyes locked with hers, and to her shame she was the first to look away. He could hardly ban her from leaving the hotel, but suppose he cancelled his appointment and insisted on spending the rest of the afternoon with her? The thought was unbearable.

With an effort she pulled herself together, finishing the wine in her glass before saying carelessly, 'As a matter of fact I thought I'd have a look over the cathedral.'

'Dressed like that?' Dark eyebrows lifted sceptically.

'Why not?' she asked, astonished. 'There's nothing improper about it.'

'In Caracas you would be expected to dress with more dignity to visit a cathedral,' he bit back. 'To cover your arms and your head. Even in the streets of the capital it is forbidden to wear shorts, and the police deal swiftly with those who break our dress codes.'

'But then this is Salisbury, not Caracas.' Anger at the rebuke brought an added sparkle to Nella's golden eyes. 'If I were in Caracas then of course I would comply with local customs, out of courtesy rather than under pain of prosecution. Here, in England, where the libido of our men is less easily inflamed than those of Latin temperament, my dress is quite proper. Rest assured, it's unlikely that I shall be struck down on the threshold of the cathedral by a thunderbolt.'

'It wasn't only thunderbolts of which I was thinking.' He smiled slightly, probably because he considered that her reference to Latin libido was some kind of compliment to his virility, she determined crossly. 'It's a hot day, and even in these colder latitudes the expanse of pale skin you are exposing to the sun could be inviting trouble of another kind.'

'Thank you,' Nella said coldly. 'I've lived with this skin for twenty-four years without inflicting damage on it. Believe me, I shall protect it amply from anything that threatens it—animal, vegetable or mineral.'

'Then with that assurance I shall have to be content.' He raised an imperious hand, gold cufflinks gleaming against the champagne silk of the shirt-cuff showing slightly beneath his jacket as he summoned the waiter. 'What do you wish for dessert?'

The remainder of the meal passed comparatively quietly as Nella concentrated on eating the strawberries soaked in Cointreau and served with cream, which had been her choice from the menu. Two cups of black coffee later, she felt more composed, although the inexorably ticking away minutes gave her some cause for alarm.

It was half-past two before the meal was finished and they were able to leave the dining-room.

'My car is outside. Can I give you a lift to the cathedral?' Raúl enquired politely on the threshold of the foyer.

'Quite unnecessary,' she murmured, anxious to escape his presence so that she could meet Michael as arranged. 'I don't want to take you out of your way.'

'You won't.' He towered over her, power emanating from every pore of his feral body beneath the elegant apparel which camouflaged it without detracting from its strength. A wolf in sheep's clothing, indeed. A small smile trembled at the corners of Nella's full mouth at the thought. 'I can drop you off nearby without having to take a detour.'

She moved uneasily, alarmed and puzzled by his insistence, afraid that he suspected she was up to something nefarious and unwilling to give substance to his suspicions. But, she consoled herself, there was a limit to the time he could spare in trying to persuade her if he didn't want to be late.

'Really, it's no problem,' she protested airily. 'I want to go back to the room and freshen up first. Besides, I shall enjoy the walk. It's not at all far.'

'Not with comfortable shoes.' His eyes lowered to regard her feet, the neatly painted geranium toenails bright against the high-heeled white sandals, distracting attention from the small pink plaster above them. 'How is your blister?'

'Practically healed,' she confirmed patiently. 'Believe me, Raúl, I'm flattered by your concern for my well-being, but I really can look after myself in normal circumstances.'

'But these circumstances are hardly normal, are they, *guapa*?' he retorted softly. 'And I feel constrained to do everything I can to ensure that Luis will not recover from his coma to find himself possessed of goods which have sustained further damage. Take care, Nella. I shall expect to see you back at the hotel by six. That will give us time to discuss our plans for the evening. I'll see you in the lounge or in our room, whichever you prefer.'

'The lounge, then.' Biting back her anger at the reference to damaged goods, she gave him a demure smile which was acknowledged by a curt move of his sable head before he turned away, striding towards the exit with his customary litheness and assurance. Whatever plans he intended making for the evening, she could only hope they'd extend well into the small hours of the morning, so that the time she'd be obliged to spend alone in the double room with him would be strictly limited.

Nella made her way cautiously to the foyer, relieved to see Raúl's back disappearing through the swing-doors as Michael rose to greet her from his vantage point beside the reception desk.

'Where would you like to talk?' He approached her easily, taking her arm gently.

'Perhaps we could stroll towards the cathedral? I told Raúl I'd probably go there this afternoon, and I don't like lying to him.'

'Whatever pleases you, Nella.' He shot her a curious look. 'You're not afraid of this guy, are you?'

'No—no, of course not!' Her denial came a little too quickly, forcing her to amplify. 'It's just that our relationship is—is a little new. Raúl's a little uncertain of my—my integrity.' She forced a bright smile to her lips. 'Let's just call it Latin American jealousy. He's no threat to me, I just care too much for him to want to upset him.'

'If you say so.' Michael looked doubtful. 'But if he wants a witness to your integrity, I'll gladly put him right in the picture!'

'Thanks, Michael. But it's really not necessary.' Quickly Nella dismissed his offer of help. 'Now, tell me what you've been doing since I last saw you.'

It was four o'clock when Michael reluctantly announced that he ought to be making his way back to the hotel. Sitting on a seat in the shadow of the cathedral, they had reminisced over old times and brought each other up to date with new ones. Although Nella had carefully avoided discussing Raúl's place in her life, dismissing their acquaintanceship as too recent to comment on.

Michael, on the other hand, had been eager to bring her up to date on his own achievements. Although he was still based at Lowdale Heath he would shortly be leaving, having decided to specialise in geriatric care and accepted a post attached to a large Midlands health authority. More exciting still, he was planning to marry in the near future—a winsome blonde nursing sister, he had informed her bashfully—although they had kept their engagement a secret until her parents returned from a six-month visit to her brother in New Zealand.

'Don't forget you're invited to the official engagement party,' he reminded Nella, taking her hand in his own as he prepared to leave her. 'I'll make it out to Miss Lambert and partner, OK?'

'OK!' She smiled. 'Do give your fiancée my congratulations for me, won't you? Tell her she couldn't have picked a nicer, kinder, more compassionate man in the whole wide world!'

'I'll tell her,' he promised. 'And I hope the man you've chosen will appreciate just what a wonderful girl he's getting too, Nella.' He gave her a lopsided smile. 'Until Carol came into my life I never thought I'd meet anyone who would matter to me as much as you did. Now I know you were right. You and I were meant to be friends, Nella, not lovers.'

He took her in his arms and kissed her fondly on each cheek. 'I'll send the party invitation to your brother's address. The seminar ends at eight, and I don't suppose I'll be seeing you again before I leave, so look after yourself and tell your "friend" that he'll have me to account to if he upsets you! Here—' he raised his hand to his lapel and detached the red rosebud which had been pinned there '—I helped myself to this from the display in the foyer while I was waiting for you—a token of our friendship.'

Tucking the stem beneath the straps of her dress, Nella watched him stride away, blinking back the tears from her eyes, overjoyed that he'd found someone to love him as much as he deserved. It had been great talking over the past, a catharsis which had washed away the last

vestiges of guilt she had felt about her inability to give
Rosie the best care available. No one, Michael had
vowed, could have achieved even half of what she had!

Sighing, she turned her attention to the cathedral.
There was plenty of time to look around before she had
to leave for her evening rendezvous with Raúl.

Emerging into the still bright sunlight an hour later, she
decided to stroll along the quiet lanes of the cathedral
close, enjoying the still perfection of the day. Just as she
was contemplating the need to turn back on her tracks
and make for the hotel, if she was not to keep Raúl
waiting, she found her steps had led her down a narrow
pathway towards a high wrought-iron gate, almost entirely overgrown with brambles and creeper, which was
embedded in a towering weatherworn brick wall. Its
hinges rusted, there remained a narrow gap through
which an intruder might squeeze if given enough mo-
tivation. Dared she trespass?

Peering through the gap, she was presented with a vista
of nature's overgrown splendour surrounding a large,
single-storeyed building, which even from a distance
showed signs of disrepair, indicating that it had been
unoccupied for a long time. Tumbles of roses, honey-
suckle and everlasting sweet-peas swung from col-
lapsing, fungus-ridden arches beneath which swayed
waist-high grasses, their seed-heads trembling in the slight
breeze, their slender stalks intermingled with scarlet
poppies and blue chicory. Eden overgrown, she thought
poetically, feasting her eyes on a panorama where bees
sucked drowsily at the purple flowers of giant hebe
shrubs and butterflies hovered above clouds of purple
and white buddleia. Surely no one would object to her
peaceful intrusion into this lush and untended paradise?

Automatically she glanced guiltily along the previously deserted path, and froze in astonishment at the sight of the tall figure advancing purposefully towards her. Despite his lack of jacket and the open-necked shirt above the pale trousers, there was no mistaking Raúl's impressive persona, which seemed to operate on a slightly higher plane than anyone else's that she'd ever met, so that everything about him was slightly larger than life—his vigour, his charisma, his sheer energy.

'Raúl!' She was the first to speak, moving forward to greet him, making no attempt to disguise her pleasure. 'You've been looking for me?'

'Not exactly. I've known your whereabouts ever since you left the hotel.' No answering smile softened the harsh set of his features, neither did he make any attempt to hide the biting contempt in his tone, which struck her as painfully as if he'd raised his hand to her.

An incredulous laugh escaped Nella's mouth, which had opened in shock at the unexpected admission. 'You've been following me?'

'You and your lover,' he confirmed, his voice edged like a scythe about to demolish a field of wheat.

A burst of hysterical laughter rose to Nella's lips. That was good. A field of wheat... Wheatley...

'Confess it, Nella. You and Michael Wheatley were in it together, weren't you? A poor country physician with ambition and a beautiful woman who could sell her attributes to help him on his way. When you met Luis all your prayers must have been answered.' The light blue eyes studied her with a piercing scrutiny. 'Marry him, steal from him, desert him—then lie low until he rid himself of you like a terrier shaking off a rat! Then it was going to be *Adiós*, Luis; *Bienvenido*, Michael!'

# CHAPTER TEN

'MICHAEL?' Her heart was beating quickly, and she could feel her palms grow damp with apprehension. How on earth had he traced Michael—and why? And, more to the point, how had he managed to distort the facts to fit some obscene scenario of his own imagination?

'How do you know about Michael?' She blurted out the question, oblivious to its potential of being regarded as a confession.

'Because I made it my business to find out!' He reached out, taking her arm to draw her close into his own body-space, his light blue eyes studying her reaction with a piercing scrutiny. 'You intrigued me, Nella. Oh, even at first I wasn't prepared to accept your denials of being Luis's wife, but there were anomalies. Even when Luis greeted you by name I couldn't be sure. When he became so disturbed, and asked that you be sent away, was it because he hated you, or was there a possibility, after all, against all the odds, that you weren't the woman he married?'

'Yes—yes, Raúl!' Eagerly she raised her free hand and clasped his forearm as relief flowed through her like a tidal wave. 'Of course, that was it! Somehow he recognised me—but *knew* I wasn't his wife!'

'Take care, *guapa*!' To her anguish he greeted her enthusiasm with contempt, thrusting her back against the wall, glowering down into her upturned face. 'I warned you once before about twisting the tail of jaguar. The questions I asked myself needed answers, and I wasn't prepared to wait. Fortunately I have a good friend in this country, a fellow undergraduate at Oxford. You may even have heard of him—Roger Charleston, one of this country's leading barristers. His contacts are powerful and widespread and he agreed instantly to organise an investigation for me.'

'But on what evidence?' Bewildered, Nella shook her head.

'Things Luis told me when he telephoned. Small pieces of disseminated information I gathered from the fragments of his letter, plus the information you yourself gave me—the name of the village in Cambridgeshire where you lived with your grandmother, for instance. What better place to find out more about you than in the place where you claimed you'd lived for two years?'

'Someone went there?' Her mind was spinning in disbelief. 'But how could you organise that so quickly?'

'Simple.' Raúl's chin rose triumphantly. 'Yesterday I had a brief but fruitful meeting with one of the top-rate investigators Roger had hired. Not only was I able to give him all the information I'd gleaned, but also to allow him the opportunity of seeing you in action—even to take a photograph of you...'

'The club you took me to last night!' Incredulity froze Nella's expression, to be followed by a wave of colour as she recalled how the evening had ended.

'Top marks for deduction,' he returned silkily as a cold knot formed in her stomach. 'Roger was indeed our sponsor for the evening, and by the time the investigator had left, he could have been in little doubt about your versatility.'

'You deliberately tried to warp his mind against me!' Furiously, but to no avail, Nella tried to detach herself from his muscular hold. 'But it won't have made any

difference. People at Lowdale Heath know me for what
I am. They were my friends! No one will have lied about
me!'

'I'm sure they didn't, *querida*.' A quick shadow of
anger swept across his face. 'First thing this morning,
my investigator was interviewing the owner of the village
shop, speaking to the local vicar, enquiring about you
from the neighbours.' He drew in a deep breath before
continuing slowly, his fingers caressing her arm in a
monotonous rhythm that echoed his words. 'You were
right, Nella. Everyone regarded you as a saint—almost
too good to be true. Everyone wished you well for the
future—your future with Michael Wheatley, the local
doctor who had tended your grandmother and whose
admiration for you outshone the rest of the community's. It was an open secret that Wheatley was engaged—
officially a secret engagement—but not one person
spoken to doubted for a moment that you were the
woman in his life.'

'That's absurd!' She heard her own voice, stiff and
unnatural. 'Michael was a friend——'

Brutally he truncated her protest. 'So our investigator
went to see the noble doctor in his surgery, only to discover that he was away on a seminar—in Salisbury.'

White-faced, Nella stared at his haughty face, her
thoughts in a turmoil.

'You didn't come here on business at all, did you?'
she gasped. 'You brought me here to confront me with
Michael? To see if what you'd been told was true?'

He didn't deny it. 'As soon as I received the telephoned report this morning, I made that decision.'

'But we might never have met...' She shook
her head distractedly. 'The place was crawling
with delegates——'

'Which is why I arranged to meet you in the bar and to have Wheatley paged for a phone call at the same time. And if that hadn't worked then I would have found another way to bring you two face-to-face.' He paused meaningfully. 'But the first plan worked, and you fell into each other's arms like lovers. And later, after lunch, I followed you, Nella. Watched you laughing and holding hands. Saw your goodbye kiss, the rose he gave you...' Lifting one hand, he flicked its damask petals as they nestled against her skin.

'When did you arrange to meet again? What plans did you make, hmm? Don't lie to me, *mujer*. Tell me what part this man has in your life—how long you've known him. Is he the one you betrayed Luis for?' His voice was low, every word taut with menace. 'I've been following you, watching you, waiting to see what you'd do next, but my patience is exhausted. I have to know the truth now.'

'Stop it, Raúl!' Enough was enough. And this was more than enough. An unexpected surge of courage forced her into defiance. 'How dare you spy on me and jump to such ridiculous and unfounded conclusions? Michael and I are friends, and, no—I'm not surprised that the gossips have linked our names together. Two years ago Michael asked me to marry him and I turned him down. I loved him as a friend—as a kind and compassionate man—but I didn't love him as I hope to love the man I eventually marry—with all my heart and soul and being!' She was breathing heavily, her voice rising and falling with emotion.

'When we met today it was a marvellous reunion. And the most marvellous thing of all was that Michael is indeed secretly engaged to be married, but not to me! The woman he loves is a nurse, and as soon as her parents

are back in this country it's going to be official. And if
you don't believe me, you can send your snooper back
to Lowdale Heath and tell him to confront Michael
direct—and, for his sake, I hope Michael doesn't punch
him on the jaw!' With an almighty effort she twisted
away from his grip, landing him a blow in the solar plexus
as she sought her freedom.

She heard him swear, low and intensely in Spanish,
felt a glow of satisfaction that she'd winded him, but
knew she had no chance of outrunning him. Neither, in
the quiet lane, was there any chance that a passer-by
would come to her aid. Only the secret garden behind
the wall held out the hope of sanctuary.

Her heart beating an urgent tattoo, she squeezed
through the half hidden entrance and ran as best she
could through the dense undergrowth, praying that Raúl
wouldn't follow her, or that if he did she'd be swift
enough to find a hiding place that would outfox him.

Her prayers went unheeded. Brambles barred her
passage and wild oats tickled the bare skin of her legs;
rambling roses caught in her hair as tendrils of wild
bryony tugged at her arms. Great clumps of larkspur
swayed at her passing, expelling pollen-soaked bumble
bees, but she fought on, blindly accompanied by the
anxious twitterings of disturbed birds and the frenzied
fluttering of butterflies, with no thought of where her
headlong flight would lead her. Tears of anger and frustration were brimming in her eyes and trickling down
her twig-and thorn-grazed cheeks, and she was conscious only that behind her, lethal as the hunting jaguar
to which he had likened himself, Raúl relentlessly
pursued her.

She was sobbing in anguish, her breath harsh in her
throat, her limbs aching with effort, when almost mir-

aculously nature's plethora of untamed vegetation gave way to a stretch of luscious green grass, no more than two metres wide, beyond which flowed the gentle waters of what she guessed must be the River Avon.

It was a comparatively narrow stretch of water, but in her agitated state she had no idea of how deep it might be and felt a cautious reluctance to find out the hard way by throwing herself into it. With a cry of despair she turned like a trapped animal, conscious only of the sudden deep silence which had descended on the afternoon, and found herself facing Raúl.

'Nella...' He came towards her, his voice hard and urgent. 'For God's sake, Nella, don't run away from me again!' His eyes raked over her as she stared back at him, her heart pounding, a multitude of dangerous sensations streaming through her. 'I don't want to hurt you... I never did...'

'Then what do you want?' She hardly recognised her own voice, detesting the way it shook but finding herself unable to control it. 'I'm tired of your unfounded accusations. I'm weary of being treated like a liar and a thief when I'm neither...' Two tears rolled down her cheeks, and she brushed them angrily away with the back of her hand. 'I only stopped protesting my innocence because I wanted some peace...'

'You're bleeding.' He took a clean handkerchief from the pocket of his shirt, took her arm gently in one hand and dabbed at her torn cheek with the spotless linen. '*Dios*! What have I done to you, *querida*?'

For the first time the endearment lacked the hard edge of sarcasm as his beautiful eyes took their toll of her anguished face.

It wasn't what she'd expected, and she drew back, stunned and puzzled, as she read once more the undeniable signs of arousal on his strong, masculine face, and felt her own awareness leap to acknowledge it.

'Raúl,' she croaked, half-protest, half-plea, her heart seeming to leap in her throat as her legs threatened to give way beneath her and she chose the safer option of slumping down on the grassy bank. He followed her down, his hands pushing her hair away from her flushed forehead, his lips trailing heated kisses across the pitted velvet of her skin, where nature's sentinels had tried in vain to prevent her passage.

'Do you want me to stop?' He whispered the question against her mouth.

Dear God, how she wanted to have the self-control to deny her own longings, to say 'yes', but the crisp blue-black darkness of his hair was lying like a jaguar's pelt within such tempting reach of her fingers as his mouth moved in tiny salutatory kisses across her jawline, and reason was fleeing before the heady sensation of his nearness. A small cry of anguish mingled with pleasure escaped her as he eased his body nearer to her own, moving one leg to imprison both of hers beneath him. The words which would have stopped him died in her throat.

How dark his eyes were! The pupils large and black, the clear blue beauty of the iris like a corona around a lifeless planet. Entranced by the thick lushness of his eyelashes, Nella was oblivious of the hand which pushed the slender straps of her sundress down her upper arms. Only when she felt his fingers, warm and predacious against the naked skin of her breast, did she make a murmur of protest, which swelled to a cry of constricted yearning as his searching fingers found and caressed the quiescent apex.

Trapped in a vortex of desire, Nella's whole body jerked in sensuous protest against the marauding fingers which teased her with their gentle touch, her mouth opening fully, the easier to accommodate Raúl's practised, penetrating kiss. She wanted him as a woman wanted the man she loved—with every beat of her heart, every fibre of her being. In an agony of indecision she realised she'd known it since that first time by the boulder beach, and had tried to force it out of her consciousness because it had been impossible. Was still impossible!

'Raúl...' She'd meant to cry his name in protest, but it dripped from her lips like honey, warm and soft... lubricating the sweetness of his kiss. Once more she tried, summoning up every atom of strength left to her. 'Raúl!'

'Hush, *querida*, I know!' He'd made his own translation of her agonised plea and moved to assuage the ache which was tormenting her, lowering himself against her body, easing her legs apart so that the lower part of his own body rested on the ground, protecting her from the full weight of its superb masculinity.

Instinctively her arms rose to caress him. Driven by a primordial need, she caught him to her, her hands moving firmly down his muscled back, following the line of his spine, enjoying the sensuous feeling of his silk shirt, until even that was not enough and she pulled mindlessly at the garment, dragging it away from his belt so that she could finger the warm satin that was his naked skin.

There was a moment of triumph, when she heard him groan and felt the full thrust of his manhood rise hard against the encompassing cradle of her body, before the full realisation of what she was doing burst upon her, awakening her from the lethargy of desire which had inundated and subdued her scruples.

With a sharp cry of distress, she responded to the self-revulsion which had returned to shame her with the agonising accuracy of a boomerang reaching its target.

This time Raúl heeded her anguish, rolling away from her, breathing heavily, his face hauntingly beautiful with the flush of arousal slashed across his high, Aztec-contoured cheekbones.

Twisting away from his slumbrous gaze, humiliatingly aware that she was naked to the waist, with shaking fingers Nella tried to pull her dress back into place, peeling away the bruised petals of the rose which had somehow become detached and plastered to her delicate skin. She could smell their heady perfume, allied to her own, and the musky scent of Raúl's sun-warmed skin— a haunting, stimulating essence that even now, in the depth of degradation, incited her senses.

She loved him—but how could she? Shivering under the harsh stricture of her conscience, she demanded an answer from herself. How could she love a man who, believing her to be married to his own brother, would attempt to seduce her . . . and not for the first time? Had she no pride at all to succumb to the accomplished caresses of a man who had more than once bitingly termed her *ramera*?

But there was no answer forthcoming from her dazed mind as somehow she struggled to her feet, her only wish now to put as much distance between herself and her tormentor as possible. But she'd only taken a few stumbling steps, her eyes blinded by tears of humiliation, when she felt his hand, a firm brake on her shoulder.

'Nella . . .'

'Let me go.' Her breath was still ragged, but she spoke the words with hauteur. 'How dare you condemn me when you wouldn't think twice about betraying your own brother?'

'Listen to me.' Quiet determination sharpened his tone.

'There's nothing you can say that I want to hear.' She tried to take another step, but his hand tightened restrainingly.

'Even if it's about you and Luis?' he insisted brutally.

'Particularly if it's about me and Luis,' she responded with an effort. 'I'm not in the mood to listen to any more of your insults.'

'Do I insult you when I tell you I believe you?'

Somewhere in Nella's heart a faint spark of hope kindled, only to be extinguished. This was another trick, a further gambit designed to entrap her. It had to be.

'Really?' She raised a querulous eyebrow as she blinked rapidly to dispel any remaining tears, determined not to flinch at whatever rejoinder she was about to invite. 'About what, in particular?'

The silence was absolute, then a thrush trilled a cadence, paused and repeated the same sequence of notes. As the echo of its call faded Raúl spoke.

'I accept that you are not the woman whom Luis married,' he said heavily.

'What?' It was little more than a whisper as Nella's hands rose to her chest and crossed against the swell of her breasts to become conscious of the increased beating of her heart, which sent a surge of blood singing to her temples. She tried to amplify her question, but found herself a victim of the temporary paralysis affecting her vocal cords.

'Oh, at first it seemed absurd that there might be a third party concerned—that anyone should have gone to such extremes as to marry Luis under another woman's name—and I wasn't prepared even to consider such a ridiculous supposition.' Raúl's gaze swept across her astonished face as he paused thoughtfully. 'But later...the more I got to know you...the more doubtful I became that you were implicated in this sorry business...' He made a helpless gesture with his hands. 'I began to suspect that you might be telling me the truth after all. Small things didn't equate with the information I'd gleaned from Luis. For instance, you could have been lying when you told me you'd studied languages——' his mouth twisted in a wry smile '—but then I remembered you'd called me a pig in Spanish. Luis's wife knew only English...'

'Go on,' she encouraged softly as he paused.

'Luis had met his wife in a bar. She'd been the life and soul of the party, according to the description he gave me when he telephoned. It was one of the reasons he noticed her in the first place. He told me she had a striking voice and was the star of the karaoke machine.' His eyes narrowed perceptively as they dwelt on her pale face. 'But you told me you couldn't sing.'

'I can't!' It was the first time the fact had delighted her. 'But I could have been lying deliberately,' she added perversely, still uncertain of his motives.

'Do you think I didn't realise that?' He released her shoulder, evidently satisfied that he was holding her full attention and physical restraint was no longer necessary to compel her presence. 'But you never showed any signs of breaking into song, and then I heard you humming tunelessly when you thought you were alone—and it was music to my ears.'

Nella smiled, it was the most charming compliment she'd ever received—but surely not conclusive?

'Go on,' she prompted eagerly.

'There were other more important things,' he continued thickly. 'Your sense of loyalty to your brother. Your knowledge of food and wine. Your general level of intelligence...' He stopped speaking and began pacing, taking a few steps, then turning and retracing them as Nella watched, transfixed.

'It could all have been an act,' she ventured, playing the devil's advocate, unwilling to believe in his sincerity until she was a hundred per cent certain of his integrity.

'Yes,' he agreed tersely. 'But I'm usually a good judge of men—and women—and my instincts were beginning to tell me you were genuine.' He paused. 'The only problem was that my judgement was clouded, because I was attracted to you physically from the first moment I saw you, and I was reluctant to trust it. Torn between loyalty to Luis and my own powerful reaction to everything about you, for the first time in my life I didn't know which way to turn—who or what to believe.'

'You chose a very effective way of forcing a confession from me at the boulder beach,' she commented wryly, still hardly able to believe what she was hearing, yet perversely flattered because he'd admitted he had found her attractive. 'Unfortunately it wasn't a true one—just a means of self-preservation.'

'May God forgive me!' He stopped striding to thump one fist into the palm of his other hand with barely controlled fury. 'It was never my intention to frighten you. There was nothing planned about what happened. You are a beautiful woman and I...' He laughed bitterly. 'I wasn't immune to that beauty. My animal instinct temporarily overruled my honour. But even if you hadn't stopped me when and as you did, I am not a barbarian that I would have continued on such a path of destruction.'

'But you said——' Nella started to protest.

'I lied to protect my own pride. In that moment of anti-climax I was hurting, physically and mentally. I'd just seen, or believed I'd seen, Luis claim you as his wife. But even then there was something about you—a core of honesty, perhaps—which I sensed, and which disrupted all logical thought, but I made myself ignore it.' He gave a brief, self-castigating laugh. 'A true son of Adam, I blamed the woman for tempting me.'

'I'd no intention of tempting anyone,' Nella said sadly. 'I was just confused about what had happened, especially when Luis knew my name.' She raised appealing hazel eyes to Raúl's face as she recalled her horror. 'I'd never seen your brother before in my life, but he called me by name. It was like a nightmare. I was stunned. At that moment I knew there was no chance of you believing me.'

'At first, no,' Raúl confessed. 'But every minute we spent together I felt my certainty about your guilt diminish. I began to search for an explanation and suddenly I remembered that when Luis had spoken to me or written about you he'd never called you Nella—it was always Rusty.'

'So that's why you called me Rusty earlier today—to test my reaction?' she asked a trifle breathlessly.

Raúl made an expressive gesture with both hands. 'And it convinced me that you'd never answered to it before. The more I thought about it, the more I began to believe that your only mistake was to bear a physical resemblance to the woman who married Luis. And that was why, when she was looking for an alias to hide her own identity, she borrowed yours.'

'Yes—yes . . .' Nella's eyes shone with the relief which was permeating her entire body. 'That would explain Luis's description of his wife——'

'And also why he was so anxious for me to send you away,' he offered thoughtfully. 'He wasn't able to tell us at the time, but somehow he'd found out that Nella and Rusty were two different people. At first he was delighted I'd found you—because somehow you hold the key to the mystery—then afterwards, when he realised I thought you were his wife, he tried to tell me to send you away—that I'd made a dreadful mistake!'

'Oh, Raúl! That must be it!' Excitedly she laughed up into his face, then felt her pleasure drain away as she remembered the cause of her headlong flight through the undergrowth. 'But if you'd already decided I was telling the truth why did you set up the meeting between me and Michael?'

Hands thrust into the pockets of his trousers, Raúl scowled at her from beneath lowered brows. 'Because I was jealous—I had to be sure. Even if you weren't married to Luis you could still have been involved with Wheatley. I had to see for myself. Then when you entered the bar, in your dress the colour of *bucare* blossom, and I saw your shining eyes and smiling mouth, I feared the worst.' He raised a hand, as if to touch the faint smear of carmine on her shoulder left on her skin by the crushed petals of the rose. 'I'd only just accepted that you were not my sister-in-law. And then, later, when I saw you together, laughing and joking, kissing . . . wearing the rose he'd given you . . .' His voice harshened. 'May God forgive me, but I made some wild and totally unjustified assumptions.'

Jealous? Why should she feel so surprised? Nella felt her heart pounding uncomfortably against her breastbone. From their first meeting she and Raúl had been victims of a powerful sexual tension which had had nothing to do with her presumed relationship with Luis. He desired her, wanted to experience and enjoy her soft body, fill her with his essence, take her with a mindless pleasure which would exhaust them both.

A warm flush of anticipation rose like a life-giving stream from the depth of her body, sharpening her awareness of him, so that everything about him seemed more powerful, more irresistible. He didn't love her— not as she loved him. But it didn't matter. His was the animal hunger of proximity, but her own well of love would be enough to dignify their union.

Her mouth dry with expectation, Nella swallowed, unable to make the first move. 'The rose came from the foyer in the hotel,' she brought out breathlessly, anxious to break the tension which shimmered between them like a tangible force. 'Michael helped himself while he was waiting for me to join him. It was nothing but a token of friendship. He just wanted to reminisce over the past and let me know of his plans to get married.' She swallowed hard, gathering her courage to ask the question she needed him to answer more than anything else in the world at that moment. 'Do you believe me, Raúl? Do you finally believe that I'm not the woman who married Luis?'

She was rewarded by a glimmer of a smile as Raúl's eyes encompassed her shapely body. It needed only one word to transport her to a seventh heaven, and he said it.

'Yes.'

Tears of relief, almost exultation, stung behind her lids as she made an effort to prevent their falling, reaching to place her eager hands on his upper arms in

a gesture of trust and happiness. How she'd longed for
the moment when she could take the high moral ground
and reduce him to less than dirt beneath her feet. But
now that moment had come she felt no desire to avenge
the heartless abduction to which he'd subjected her, only
this overwhelming need to touch him, to be close to him.

'Raúl,' she whispered, hoping that he would read the
message in her eyes.

Abruptly, cruelly, he detached her hands from his
body. 'You're quite right, Nella. Come—it's time we
went.' Brusquely his deep voice penetrated her thoughts,
destroying the images she'd been building. 'We'll have
an early dinner at the hotel and leave immediately
afterwards.'

'Where for?' An unwelcome premonition threatened
her euphoria.

'Back to your brother's house, of course.' He slanted
her a surprised look. 'The abductor returns his victim—
unharmed. Where else?'

'But—I thought—I mean...' Stammering, she lowered
her eyes before his steady stare. 'Now you accept that
I've never had anything to do with your brother...' She
bit her lip self-consciously, then persevered painfully as
the colour flooded her pale cheeks. 'I mean, you booked
the room for the night, didn't you?'

A harsh bark of laughter greeted her equivocation.
'An action you objected to quite strongly at the time, I
seem to remember. If it was unseemly then it appears to
be even more unseemly now—no?'

'No—yes...' Her world of romance was disinte-
grating before her and she had to make a determined
effort to pull herself together. It seemed that now Raúl
had finally accepted she was not the woman who'd en-

snared his brother her forbidden charm had evaporated, and he wanted nothing more to do with her.

He shrugged wide shoulders. 'Then there's nothing to keep us here any longer. Come. I promised my mother that I'd ring her this afternoon to get the latest bulletin on Luis.'

Biting back her chagrin and disappointment, Nella went. This time Raúl led, cleaving a path through the tangle of foliage and flowers, and she followed in his wake. The sun had disappeared behind a cloud, and what had appeared like a blooming oasis when she had first peered through the gate now took on the aspect of a dreary, overgrown patch of wasteland.

Clearly she'd read too much into his avowal of jealousy. It had been impersonal—a natural predator's reaction to a stranger on his patch. He hadn't wanted her to show an interest in any other man, but it didn't mean that he cared sufficiently about her to want to make love to her. It had simply been enough for him to confirm that she would have been a willing victim to his own personal brand of seduction, and he pursued it, before rejecting her.

As they approached the rusted wrought-ironwork of the concealed gate she felt a pang of sympathy for the biblical figure of Eve. Now she, too, humiliated and regretful, knew what it was like to be denied paradise.

# CHAPTER ELEVEN

THE pre-dinner cocktail party was in full swing. Sipping her dry sherry, Nella smiled politely at the earnest young man who was once more extolling her brother's virtues to her.

'Of course,' he was saying enthusiastically, 'we always knew that barring some unforeseen catastrophe David was bound to be elected!'

'Fortunately, Peter, that didn't occur. The catastrophe, I mean.' Nella returned his smile with a wry twist of her lips, delighted that David had been elected by a comfortable margin of votes.

'Ah!' Her companion helped himself to another glass of sherry from the silver tray of a circulating waitress. 'I see what you mean! Rum do, that foreigner turning up and claiming that you'd had some dodgy relationship with his brother. Could have caused a nasty scandal at an inappropriate time. Lucky you were able to convince him otherwise.'

Nella sighed. 'Yes, it was. But I'm not too keen on the papers getting hold of the story.' She cast him an admonitory look. 'If you hadn't been here when Raúl brought me back...'

'I wouldn't have known anything about it!' He gave her a cheeky grin. 'Don't worry. You can trust me not to breathe a word—although I don't see how you'll be able to keep it quiet when that woman—what's her name?—comes up for trial.'

'Rusty—Rusty Naylor,' she reminded him. 'Hopefully, when the bigamy case comes to court, it will be sufficient to state that she used another name on the marriage certificate without having to say that it was mine. It's not as if she intends to fight the case, and fortunately it means that the marriage was totally illegal.' She gave him a polite smile. 'Now, if you'll excuse me—I really should circulate...'

Easing herself away from his eager presence in a drift of cream and bronze voile, she kept the sociable smile pasted to her face as she mingled with David and Charmian's guests at the party they were throwing as a thank-you for their supporters after the successful by-election result. It was to be the last social gathering David would host for some time now as he buckled down to deal with his new responsibilities.

Dear David, she thought whimsically, he'd done everything he could to get the mystery investigated without delay. It wasn't his fault that in the end it had been Raúl who had solved the mystery.

Refusing another glass of sherry, and confident that all the guests were happily in conversation, she slipped out of the crowded room to take refuge halfway up the imposing flight of stairs which led to the small, mock minstrel-gallery.

It was cooler here, away from the mass of bodies downstairs. Wearily she slumped against the banisters, admitting to herself that she was finding it difficult to enter wholeheartedly into the celebrations. Inevitably her thoughts returned to Raúl. It was over a week since he'd returned to Caracas, with a rapidly recovering Luis and the rest of his family, leaving a gap in her life she was finding it hard to fill. Now all the fuss of the by-election was over she'd have to start searching seriously for a property she could afford to buy—as well as a full-time job. If only she could feel a little more animated over the prospects of the new life awaiting her!

The after-effects of shock, Charmian had suggested, sweetly sympathetic and untypically affectionate when she'd been made privy to the whole story. And it had been a shock, Nella admitted, fingering the beautiful randomly printed voile which fell in flattering layers over her slender body.

Pearl Naylor—'Rusty' Naylor! Despite the anguish she'd been caused, Nella couldn't help smiling at the apposite nickname. It had been Raúl who had descended on the camp like an avenging god, demanding to see a register of staff employed there at the same time as she, herself. Raúl who had taken it upon himself to question the other employees, collecting a short-list of girls with shades of red hair. Raúl who had pounced on the surname 'Naylor'.

She smiled reflectively. All her information on the matter had come through David. Since that evening when, stony-faced and haughtily repentant, Raúl had delivered her into David's keeping, she'd seen him only once more. What had passed between the two men after she'd sought the sanctuary of her own bedroom she had never learned. Some inner instinct alone told her that Raúl had taken on the burden of discovering her impersonator as a penance for his harsh treatment of her as much as to avenge Luis.

Once he'd identified Pearl Naylor, and discovered she'd been employed as a domestic cleaner with access to the offices where the personnel files were kept, he'd reported the whole matter to the police. It had been a simple matter for them to trace her present whereabouts through National Insurance records, and, faced with

evidence of a badly forged signature on the marriage
register and at the bank, plus, of course, Luis's identi-
fication of her as the woman who'd stood beside him at
the register office, she'd confessed to the deception
without a struggle.

It had been a sad little story, starting innocently
enough and born of impulse. Pearl—or Rusty, as she
had been known—had found herself attracted to the
young Venezuelan, with his lust for enjoyment and the
cash to indulge it. All she'd wanted at the start was a
brief affair and a good time, she'd told the interrogating
officer in self-justification. It had been Luis who'd been
so infatuated he'd insisted on marriage, tempting her
with promises of designer clothes, jewellery, and money
to fritter away as she pleased. But marriage had been
impossible for Pearl, because she'd already got a
husband—serving a two-year sentence in prison!

She'd refused him, but Luis had insisted, stubbornly
refusing to leave her alone until eventually he'd dangled
the final bait, offering to open a bank account in their
joint names as proof of his devotion if only she would
marry him. The temptation had been too much. It was
then she'd realised that if she could get her hands on
someone else's birth certificate she could falsify the
marriage declaration. Nella, whom she'd seen on duty
in the children's play-park, had been the obvious choice.
Not only was she the right age, and unmarried, but all
her details were in the personnel folder in the office to
which Pearl, in her role of cleaner, had access.

She'd planned her disappearance, confident that Luis
wouldn't have the time or resources to search for her,
that he'd conceal the blow to his pride and cut his losses.
She'd shrugged her shoulders philosophically as she'd
confessed to her actions. How could she have foreseen

Luis's mad dash across the country and consequent accident—let alone the appearance of his brother, bent on vengeance?

Despite the trouble Rusty had caused, Nella couldn't help feeling a pang of pity for her. The police had found all the money she'd stolen from Luis packed in a paper bag at the back of a cupboard—awaiting her husband's release from gaol. It seemed that despite her desire to enjoy life to the full she still loved the man she'd legally married.

Nella sighed, clasping her arms round her bent knees as she listened to the light music emanating from the reception room. Soon dinner would be served, and she'd forgotten to ask Charmian the name of the man with whom she was to be paired. Not Peter, this time. She couldn't control the wicked smile which twitched at her lips. Apparently he'd accepted defeat in that quarter.

Poor Luis! Nella's thoughts circled back to their previous track, remembering the young man's face when she'd last seen him, nearly two weeks ago, pale and remorseful in the hospital. At least he'd made a full recovery from his physical injuries, and although his heart and pride might be scarred, he'd had the consolation of having had the money entrusted to him returned.

Lowering her head to rest on her knees, she closed her eyes, visualising the memory of that day Raúl had telephoned to tell her that Luis had recovered full consciousness, had been pronounced fit to see visitors and was eager to speak to her. Of course she'd complied with the request, her pulse increasing its beat at the prospect of seeing Raúl once more, even for such a short period of time.

He'd come to collect her and her heart had leapt like a spawning salmon the moment she'd set eyes on his toughly handsome face. She'd expected friendship but she'd received politeness; she'd wanted his approval but she'd had to settle for his courtesy. They could have been strangers as they'd walked, together but apart, down the corridor towards Luis's room.

'Nella—Raúl found you!' It was the same greeting he'd given her that dreadful day when her life had come crashing down about her ears. Scarcely aware of the elegant, dark-haired woman resting in a chair by the window, Nella had seated herself on the bed.

'You know who I am?' she'd asked breathlessly, a faint spur of fear threatening her equanimity, though she knew she'd never set eyes on Luis Farrington in her life before that first traumatic meeting in hospital.

'Of course.' His smile had been warm, in direct opposition to the icily etched lines of Raúl's strong mouth. 'When I got back to my apartment and found Rusty had deserted me, I started writing a letter to Raúl, telling him what a fool I'd made of myself, but it was no good. I needed action. So I drove down to Seabeach, hoping I'd be able to trace Rusty through the holiday camp where she'd told me she worked.'

He paused, his eyes flickering shut as though in pain. 'As soon as I walked into the reception area I knew something was dreadfully wrong. There was a young woman there, sorting through a pile of posters, and suddenly there was the name of the woman I'd married. "Nella Lambert—employee of the month!" The name was fine, but not the face!'

'Oh!' Instantly she realised the shock he must have received, remembered her own pleasure in being given the honour—her name on the poster beneath a large and full-colour portrait taken by the camp photographer.

'I knew then that I'd been taken for a fool.' Luis opened his eyes and regarded her steadily. 'I hoped that if I could find you, the real Nella Lambert, you might be able to help me find Rusty. I reckoned that if she knew you well enough to use your name you would know who she was.' He shrugged his shoulders beneath the silk pyjama jacket. 'I persuaded the girl behind the desk to let me have your address, and I was on the way to see you when I had the accident.'

'So when you heard a woman's voice and opened your eyes——'

'I knew who you were.' He nodded his head, drawing her eyes to the soft length of his dark hair. 'I thought you and Raúl were working together to trace Rusty for me, that everything would be all right after all.'

'Touching faith!' Raúl's clipped tones disparaged the compliment, but there was a gruffness in his voice which betrayed the fondness he felt for the younger man, and an affection which would outlast his brother's feckless behaviour.

Luis smiled wryly. 'Then I realised he thought *you* were my wife, and I tried to tell him that you weren't, only I wasn't strong enough...' He glanced across at Raúl's stern face, adding ingenuously, 'But in the end it didn't matter. He found that out for himself.'

'Thank you for coming, my dear.' The other occupant of the room rose to her feet, extending her hand to clasp Nella's with great warmth. 'It seems that both my sons have been responsible for giving you much heartache. I can only pray that you find it in your heart to forgive them for the ordeal you've been forced to face.'

How much had Raúl confessed to his mother? There was nothing on his set face which gave her a clue, but Señora Farrington was continuing, in stilted English which it seemed she must have rehearsed many times, 'You must come and visit us in Caracas. You will always be welcome in my house and that of my son.' To Nella's astonishment she leant forward and bestowed a swift, light kiss on each of her cheeks.

Shortly afterwards Raúl had driven her home. The journey had progressed in silence and he'd politely rejected her invitation that he join her for lunch. She'd heard nothing further from him until the brief letter over a week ago, posted at Heathrow, informing her that he and his family were returning to Caracas and wishing her well.

It had been an anti-climactic ending to a drama which had demanded a final big production scene, she assessed wryly, blinking away a bead of moisture in her eye, too small to qualify as a tear, as the background music was interrupted by the loud and persistent echo of the doorbell. A late guest, perhaps?

Pulling herself to her feet, she negotiated the stairs carefully, conscious of her high-heeled sandals and the fabric of her dress swaying about her shapely legs as she made her way to the door and opened it.

'Raúl!' Her hand went open-palmed to her heart as she felt the blood drain from her face. She must be hallucinating. 'You're in Caracas!' she accused him wildly, blinking her eyelids rapidly, as if to dispel the immaculate vision dressed in an open-necked indigo sports shirt belted into leanly tailored black trousers, in order to return to reality.

'I am?' His dark eyebrows rose in mock surprise. 'Then I must be dreaming, because I could have sworn I was back in England after escorting my family safely back to Venezuela and seeing Luis happily settled for his continuing convalescence in my mother's house, where he will undoubtedly continue to be spoiled by unfailing feminine attention.'

'You sound bitter.' Her arms longed to enfold him, her mouth ached for his kiss, but her rigid self-control ensured that not a hint of her emotions showed in her normally expressive face.

'Envious,' he corrected her, his beautiful eyes gazing at her as if to strip away the invisible shield she'd erected around herself as an instinctive gesture of protection against his potent virility. 'Are you going to invite me in, or must I produce my official invitation?'

'You mean, David and Charmian are expecting you?' Somehow she must get a grip on herself, but her head was spinning, and her intellect felt sorely impaired.

'Something about not having a suitable partner for you and to the effect that Charmian's seating-plans would look untidy.' He crossed the threshold as Nella drew back automatically to allow him access. 'But it occurs to me that I may not be suitably dressed for the occasion,' he continued cheerfully, 'so perhaps it would be better if we solve the problem of matching pairs by going somewhere else.'

'Where do you suggest?' Nella enquired faintly, her mouth strangely dry, the quickened rhythm of her pulse a distracting presence in the slender column of her neck. If this was a dream then she had no wish to emerge from it.

'I still have the lease of the cottage,' he told her, the timbre of his voice even deeper than she remembered. 'I thought we might drive out there. Besides, you left some of your things there.'

The nightdress, the underclothes, the perfume... Nella shivered. 'They weren't mine. You bought them for Luis's wife!'

'I bought them for Nella Farrington,' he corrected her softly, pushing the front door closed and drawing her gently into his arms, his eyes taking their toll of her stunned expression.

'But that's not me. I mean——'

'But it could be! I want it to be.' His fingers tightened against her body, impressing their imprint on her back through the delicate voile of her dress as his voice thickened. 'Surely you know how I feel about you? From the moment I first saw you I've been haunted by your beauty, tormented by the twin devils of desire and shame because I thought for a while that you belonged to Luis! I love you, Nella. I love you because you are beautiful and eminently desirable; because you are compassionate and sincere. I love you for the way you devoted two years of your young life to care for a disorientated old lady, and for the way in which you rehabilitated yourself afterwards by seeking the innocent company of children. I love you because of your freedom from guile and because your body yields so sweetly to me, only to withdraw in confusion when I take you too far and too fast for propriety...'

'Raúl...' Held hard against his body, a surge of warmth tingling through every fibre of her being as she reacted to the potency of his words, Nella could hardly believe what she was hearing.

'But you didn't want me!' she protested. 'That afternoon at Salisbury, you must have known that I would go back to the hotel with you... I told you as much...' Heat flared to her cheeks as she remembered how blatantly she had invited his seduction, and how desolate she had felt when he had rejected the offer, insisting on taking her back to her brother's house.

'Of course I wanted you, *enamorada*,' he corrected her with a wry smile. 'Only another man would know what the effort of refusing to make love to you cost me. Only, perhaps, another Latin man would understand that it was because I love you as much as I desire to possess you, that it was essential for me to do so.' He sighed. 'We guard our women's virtue as we would the most valuable asset we hold.'

'But I wasn't your woman,' Nella teased provocatively, her mouth curved sweetly, her eyes ablaze with the love she no longer needed to hide. 'And you're not entirely Latin, are you?'

'Neither am I in the mood for contention,' he warned her mockingly. 'But the first of your objections I intend to overrule, and the second I am content to live with. So much so that I mean to increase that small percentage of non-Latin blood in my own children.'

'Children?' Nella clung to his upper arms as a fleeting vision of herself heavy with Raúl's child sped across the screen of her mind.

'In time,' he agreed. 'But not before I have introduced you to the many beauties of my country and you regard it as your first home. Although, naturally, England will always be our second home.'

Nella laughed, a sound between mirth and hysteria. 'You appear to have taken it for granted that I'll marry you,' she managed to murmur, her thighs seeking his, her breasts erotically crushed against his hard chest as all the pain of the last days evaporated.

'No, no, *querida*.' He purred the endearment, lending it an enchantment she'd never heard before. 'But as an honest woman you will find it difficult, I think, to deny that from our first meeting there was a dangerous current of attraction between us, and as a compassionate one you will understand and forgive all the sins I have committed against you, and for which I intend to make reparation for all the remaining days of my life, if you will let me.'

If she would let him! Too dazed with happiness, Nella could even forgive the arrogance of his proposal. If he'd been less sure of himself, less strong in his need to avenge his brother, she could not have loved him so much.

'But in case it is necessary to give you some positive proof of my intention not to take no for an answer,' he was continuing softly, 'I brought you this. Here...'

Reaching into his trouser pocket, he produced a jeweller's box, flipping open the lid to reveal a ring so exquisite that it took Nella's breath away.

'The three emeralds are Colombian,' he told her huskily. 'Arguably the best for depth of colour, clarity and cut, and the gold is Venezuelan, as pure as you will find anywhere in the world and, by law, only minimally adulterated by alloy. But if you don't like it...'

'It's beautiful.' Her voice shaking, Nella lifted her left hand and allowed him to slide the jewel on her finger.

'Then your answer is yes?' he demanded eagerly.

'Did you ever really doubt it?' She took a deep breath, for, having read in his magnificent eyes that one moment of fleeting doubt, she knew she had to open her heart to him. 'I love you, Raúl,' she told him simply. 'I love your passion and your pride. I love your loyalty and your persistence...' Her voice broke, but she continued bravely. 'When I received your card saying you'd returned to Caracas I thought my heart would break.'

Strain tightened the skin across his cheekbones and jaw, bringing the cleft in his chin into stark relief. 'I had to go, *querida*.' His eyes begged her understanding. 'Not only did I have to see my family safely home in the rather unusual circumstances, but I had to give you a chance to recover from your own trauma. I had given you every reason to hate me, and I had to hope, to pray, that you could find it in your heart to understand and forgive me, to remember the good moments we shared—and forget the bad.'

'What bad ones?' Nella murmured, lifting her face towards his, inviting his kiss, granting him her forgiveness with an overflowing heart...

Minutes later, he was disengaging himself from her arms, his face flushed, his voice curdled with barely suppressed desire. 'We can't stay here, my darling, or we'll create another scandal your brother can well do without!'

'The cottage, then,' Nella agreed, her eyes shining with love and happiness. 'I'll just let Charmian know she'll have to rearrange the dining-table.'

The air was balmy, the atmosphere electric as Raúl paused on the threshold of the cottage to sweep Nella into his arms and transport her up the stairs, choosing the room she'd previously slept in alone. She was only vaguely aware that the nightdress he had bought her still lay neatly folded on the pillow as he tumbled her on to the bed, following her down in the same movement, to encompass her aching body with his urgent masculine frame. His mouth was seeking hers with unspoken passion and she responded, her lips parting feverishly to accept and welcome his possessive kiss.

Her body moulded to his, fused by the mounting desire which encapsulated them both in its thrall, and her arms entwined round his neck in passionate abandon. All the reservations she'd felt, all the barriers she'd erected in the past for her own protection, crumbled and melted as his hungry kisses devoured her, sipping at her eyes, her nose, the pale damask of her cheek and the rich rose of her lips as if he would ingest her very soul into his own psyche.

She sank willingly into the mattress as his warm weight moved above her, and his mouth forsook her own to seek solace in the pale, yielding skin of her throat and shoulders, where they were exposed above the soft neckline of her dress.

There was no embarrassment, only a euphoric sensation of joy as his urgent fingers pushed the flimsy voile downwards, exposing the creamy skin of her breasts with a strangled cry of satisfaction and admiration.

'Your body is as beautiful as the rest of you,' he told her breathlessly, his fingers moving with gentle haste to undo the small line of buttons which foiled his purpose. Then his hands were sliding masterfully down to her waist, to her hips, drawing the gauzy fabric of her dress with them, until it bunched at her knees and she kicked it free, imprisoning the man she loved with her long legs, binding him to her so that the sensitive core of her body lifted to meet and welcome the awesome power of his own arousal.

Raúl's laboured breathing told her of the effort he was making to control his hunger as, with fingers which trembled, he brushed aside the thin straps of the ecru-coloured bodyshaper which was her only remaining garment. Naked beneath him, achingly aware of the leashed power of his magnificent body, for the first time Nella felt a tremor of apprehension, which reflected in the dilated pupils of her widened eyes.

'Trust me, *enamorada* . . .' The words travelled on his sweet breath as lightly as the butterflies had flitted in the garden where he had first avowed his faith in her. 'I will give you all the time you need . . .'

Tenderly, sensuously, he began to stroke her, pleasuring her with intimate caresses until her nervousness dissolved, to be replaced with a rapturous need which greeted each new intimacy with a response so eager that Raúl cried out her name as if it was an invocation to Eros himself.

'Please,' she whispered, when the torment of denial became too strong to bear, and she thought she might die unsatisfied. 'Please, *mi querido*, please...'

She was ready for him, but even so she was unprepared for the savage power of his intrusion, a thin wail of shock escaping her open mouth as he penetrated the velvet fastness of her body, stealing her chastity, branding her internally and forever with the seal of his love.

Then pleasure overtook confusion, and she found herself moving to his rhythm, her body thrusting forward to engulf him, withdrawing to tempt him and thrusting again, while her hair spread like textured silk on the pale duvet beneath them...

'I hurt you. I hurt you!' He was leaning over her, his face carved with lines of remorse as he seized her hand and pressed it to his mouth, holding her small palm against his lips, his head bowed in sorrow. '*Dios* forgive me! I should have been more patient, more mindful of your innocence...'

With an effort Nella gathered her shattered senses together. She felt replete; after all the turmoil in her life she was complete at last. No longer alone, but part of a union which she knew instinctively would go from strength to strength, conquering any adversity in its path. A new life, a new country... She could cope with anything with Raúl at her side, loving her.

'My love,' she whispered, her voice still tremulous with the after-effects of passion sated. 'Oh, my love ... Don't you know the only way you could possibly hurt me would be to leave me again?'

'Then I never shall,' he assured her resolutely, relinquishing her hand as he slid his naked body off the bed. 'At least,' he qualified, with a new lift to his deep voice, 'only for a few moments, so I can fetch the champagne and canapés I persuaded my future sister-in-law to provide me with earlier today.'

'You charmed Charmian into parting with some of her party-pieces?' Nella sat up, her hair clouding like a shawl around her ivory shoulders. She'd been so intent on the pleasures of her own initiation into the art of love that she hadn't even noticed when or how her instructor had divested himself of his own clothing. At least she could repair that omission by watching him replace it!

But Raúl seemed in no hurry to oblige her. Instead he covered his splendid nudity with a silk dressing-gown which ended mid-thigh, before bending over her and planting a small kiss on the tip of her nose.

'You'd be surprised how charming I can be, *querida*, when I put myself out. But you shall soon find out. For instance, I'm prepared to take time off work to stay here and help you arrange our wedding without delay, and afterwards to spend a long and leisurely honeymoon with you on the island of Margarita. In fact, the way I feel now, I may never work again. Somehow the prospect of devoting my time to my wife, and in due course our children, seems far more attractive than tramping through the jungle wearing a hard hat.' He threw her a mocking glance as he left the room on his self-imposed task of foraging.

He was joking, of course. Raúl Farrington would never totally forsake the challenges and satisfaction of labour, and neither would she wish him to. Leaning back on the pillow, Nella sighed rapturously, her imagination captured by the promised joys of Margarita. She knew that whatever surprises lay ahead for her she would always love this man, who had subjected her to a temporary, unfair and heartless abduction, but who had, in the final reckoning, abducted her heart on a permanent basis.

# MILLS & BOON

## Stories of love you'll treasure forever...

Popular Australian author Miranda Lee brings you a
brand new trilogy within the Romance line–
**Affairs to Remember**.

Based around a special affair of a lifetime, each
book is packed full of sensuality with some
unusual features and twists along the way!

This is Miranda Lee at her very best.

Look out for:

A Kiss To Remember in February '96
A Weekend To Remember in March '96
A Woman To Remember in April '96

# GET 4 BOOKS AND A MYSTERY GIFT

Return this coupon and we'll send you 4 Mills & Boon Romances and a mystery gift absolutely FREE! We'll even pay the postage and packing for you.

We're making you this offer to introduce you to the benefits of Reader Service: FREE home delivery of brand-new Mills & Boon romances, at least a month before they are available in the shops, FREE gifts and a monthly Newsletter packed with information.

Accepting these FREE books and gift places you under no obligation to buy, you may cancel at any time, even after receiving just your free shipment. Simply complete the coupon below and send it to:

MILLS & BOON READER SERVICE, FREEPOST, CROYDON, SURREY, CR9 3WZ.

## No stamp needed

Yes, please send me 4 free Mills & Boon Romances and a mystery gift. I understand that unless you hear from me, I will receive 6 superb new titles every month for just £1.99* each postage and packing free. I am under no obligation to purchase any books and I may cancel or suspend my subscription at any time, but the free books and gifts will be mine to keep in any case. (I am over 18 years of age)

1EP6R

Ms/Mrs/Miss/Mr _____

Address _____

_____

_____ Postcode _____

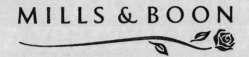

# MILLS & BOON

## Next Month's Romances

Each month you can choose from a wide variety of romance with Mills & Boon. Below are the new titles to look out for next month.

| | |
|---|---|
| ANGRY DESIRE | Charlotte Lamb |
| THE VALENTINE CHILD | Jacqueline Baird |
| THE UNFAITHFUL WIFE | Lynne Graham |
| A KISS TO REMEMBER | Miranda Lee |
| GUARDIAN GROOM | Sandra Marton |
| PRIVATE DANCER | Eva Rutland |
| THE MARRIAGE SOLUTION | Helen Brooks |
| SECOND HONEYMOON | Sandra Field |
| MARRIAGE VOWS | Rosalie Ash |
| THE WEDDING DECEPTION | Kay Thorpe |
| THE HERO TRAP | Rosemary Badger |
| FORSAKING ALL OTHERS | Susanne McCarthy |
| RELENTLESS SEDUCTION | Kim Lawrence |
| PILLOW TALK | Rebecca King |
| EVERY WOMAN'S DREAM | Bethany Campbell |
| A BRIDE FOR RANSOM | Renee Roszel |